THE FROG PRINCE
&
OTHER STORIES

THE FROG PRINCE
&
OTHER STORIES

Edited & Introduced by

TAHIR SHAH

The Scheherazade Foundation

The Scheherazade Foundation CIC
85 Great Portland Street
London
W1W 7LT
United Kingdom
www.SF.Charity
info@SF.Charity

First published by The Scheherazade Foundation CIC, 2023

THE FROG PRINCE
&
OTHER STORIES

The Frog Prince
Household Tales by the Brothers Grimm
Jacob & Wilhelm Grimm
George Bell & Sons
1884

The Buffalo & the Fieldmouse
*Wigwam Evenings Sioux Folk Tales
Retold*
Charles Alexander Eastman & Elaine
Goodale Eastman
Little, Brown, & Co.
1909

Why the Sun & the Moon Live in the
Sky
Folk Stories from Southern Nigeria
Elphinstone Dayrell
Longmans, Green & Co.
1910

The Little Settlement
Folk Tales of Breffny
Thomas G. Thrum
Macmillan & Co.
1912

Fatima's Deliverance
The Oriental Story Book
Wilhelm Hauff
D. Appleton & Co.
1855

How the Speckled Hen Got Her
Speckles
Fairy Tales from Brazil
Elsie Spicer Eells
E.M. Hale & Co.
1917

The Old Woman & the Crooked
Sixpence
Title: Folk-lore & legends: English
Charles John Tibbits
W.W. Gibbings.
1890

How the Peacock Got His Beautiful
Feathers
Folk-Tales of the Khasis
K. U. Rafy
Macmillan & Co.
1920

The Legend of St. Bartholomew
Tales from the Lands of Nuts & Grapes
Charles Sellers
Field & Tuer
1888

Simon, the Friend of Snakes
The Golden Maiden & Other Folk Tales
& Fairy Stories Told in Armenia
A. G. Seklemian
The Helman-Taylor Co.
1898

The Ungrateful Children & the Old
Father Who Went to School Again
Cossack Fairy Tales & Folk Tales
George G. Harrap & Co.
1916

The Beautiful Daughter of Liu-Kung
Chinese Folk-lore Tales
Rev. J. Macgowan
Macmillan & Co.
1910

Billy Duffy & the Devil
Welsh Fairy-Tales & Other Stories
P. H. Emerson
D. Nutt Ltd.
1894

Prince Hyacinth & the Dear Little
Princess
Boys & Girls Bookshelf Folk-Lore,
Fables, & Fairy Tales
Madame LePrince de Beaumont
The University Society
1920

The various authors listed above assert the right to be identified as the Authors of the Work in accordance with the Copyright, Designs and Patents Act 1988. A CIP catalogue record for this title is available from the British Library.

ISBN 978-1-915311-08-5

CONTENTS

Series Introduction

FROM EARLIEST CHILDHOOD, I was told stories.

Of course I was – most children are told stories.

After all, telling children stories is one of the foundations that makes their early experiences a childhood.

But as I think back to the first years of my own life, I find myself reeling from the sheer quantity of stories my infant ears took in.

Whereas other children my age were told stories for amusement, my parents (and the people they associated with) recounted the endless streams of tales for a different reason.

In their opinion, stories – and the ability to tell them – were part of an ancient alchemy... a way of processing complex ideas, of solving problems, and of developing the human mind.

My father, the writer and thinker Idries Shah, believed that folklore was the single most important breakthrough ever developed by the human species. The way he saw it, the rise of stories was as consequential as the development of the languages in which they were told.

He would say that, without stories and storytelling, humanity would never have evolved in the way that it

1

has – and that the folktales, which form a bedrock of ancient societies, are more precious than any physical artefact unearthed on an archaeological dig.

As the years of my own childhood slipped by, I found myself unbothered to work out the hidden layers within treasuries of stories – what my father called 'instruction manuals to the world'. Like everyone else, I simply absorbed the individual tales, delighting in them.

And that's it – the key point, the genius of stories and storytelling.

It's a thing I only grasped in adulthood... something that fascinates me deeply.

In the same way you can jump into a car and drive across the country without giving a second thought to the engine or how it works, you can appreciate stories without understanding the hidden layers and devices that make them what they are.

Stories are all around us.

They're in the TV and movies we so adore, in the video games we play, and of course in the books we read. They're in newspapers and magazines, too; in the conversations we share with old friends, and with new ones. They're on our mobile phones, in aeroplanes, in submarines, and even in our dreams.

Our obsession with, and craving for, stories rests squarely with the way we are so absorbed by them, just as it does with the way we don't need to continually consider how and why they work.

Throughout my life, I've devoted an increasing amount of time to gathering stories from all corners of the world.

It began in my late teens, when I began to criss-cross the continents in a crazed preoccupation with folklore. I developed a first-hand love affair with societies that, over millennia, gave birth to their own astonishing traditions of stories and storytelling.

Most of the time, when reading or listening to stories, we forget that these tales have been shaped through the passage of time. Like pebbles in a river smoothed by rushing waters, they were honed through centuries of telling and retelling.

When I was twelve years old, my father published a masterwork, *World Tales*. The first edition was very large and featured hundreds of original illustrations. The book was unlike any that had come before, for it detailed the provenance and history of each story told.

At bedtime one night, he presented me with an advanced copy. For as long as I could remember, my father had been talking about the project.

Having an actual copy in my hands at last was thrilling beyond words.

Peering down at me sternly, my father said:

'This is far more than a book, Tahir Jan. It's the foundation stone of a great building... a building that *is* human culture. As you grow older, and as you go out into the world, you will understand that the folklores contained between the covers of *World Tales* have brought amusement and educated, and have solved problems when they were needed most of all.'

My father was right.

When I eventually headed out into the wilds of the world for the first time, I discovered the stories contained in *World Tales* for myself, along with a great many more. Just as he said, the stories published in his treasury were the warp and weft threads of society. Stories are the matrix on which culture itself is based – a framework that enables daily life to continue as smoothly as it does.

In this series of books, we have drawn together stories from all over the world. It's a mission begun decades ago by *World Tales*.

Some of the pieces will be known to you, and others will not.

Some will be easy to comprehend, while others will be challenging, or even nonsensical.

I'd now like to note something else...

The Occidental world seems to assume stories must appear in certain regimented ways – presented with a well-defined beginning, a middle, and an end. You know what I mean: the protagonist winning against all odds, and the happy ending to it all.

In the ancient tradition of teaching stories, the kind recounted for an eternity around campfires in the desert and in longhouses deep in the jungle, there's no such standardisation.

Rather, there's usually a hotchpotch of conflicting threads: stories without a straight linear narrative but with an underlying turbulence that gets the reader, or the listener, to sit up and think.

At The Scheherazade Foundation, we are preoccupied with the way we can extract knowledge from stories – either deliberately, or in a less structured way.

We hold the firm opinion that, in order to remove the marrow from the bone stories are best served up in the way as they were passed from one generation to the next throughout human history.

In this series, we have drawn together tales that were gathered in particular during the nineteenth and early twentieth centuries. Spanning a vast range of cultures, they offer an extraordinary glimpse into the societies from which they are drawn – societies that were often changed shortly afterwards by social upheaval, technologies, and war.

Indeed, the fact any of them were recorded at all is a thing of wonder.

Intriguingly, some of the tales will now appear dated because vocabulary and writing styles have altered. But the fact that they seem old-fashioned is of great interest – proof of the way stories are constantly changing and evolving from one era to the next.

Over the last thirty years, I've gathered hundreds of tales on my own journeys, most of them spoken directly into my ears by storytellers and fellow travellers, by wizened old men in the middle of nowhere, and by anyone else good enough to indulge my pleas.

On all those zigzagging adventures, one story sticks out, tantalising me whenever I turn it around my head.

It was called 'The Man Who Turned into a Cat'.

The reason I mention it here is not because it was an especially fine tale, but rather because, from that moment, it affected the way I perceive the world.

It was as though I were a lock and that, by hearing the tale, a key had been slipped into me and turned.

Since first receiving it, I've never been quite the same, my state of consciousness having been flipped inside out.

The fellow traveller who recounted 'The Man Who Turned into a Cat' was lost in shadow, no more than a fragment of his left cheek protruding shyly into the light.

We were sitting on low divans in a teahouse in the ancient Afghan city of Herat.

When the tale had been whispered, I sat there in silence for a long while.

'What have you done to me?' I asked after a long pause.

The fellow traveller offered half a smile.

'*I* didn't do anything,' he replied. 'It's the story that's affected you – a story that I myself first heard when I was a child playing in the orchards of Balkh.'

Peering into the shadow, my eyes widened.

'I don't understand,' I said feebly. 'After all, it's not an especially grand story. There wasn't even a jinn.'

The traveller's mouth eased out from the shadows.

Very slowly, it grinned.

'Tales containing the greatest sustenance for a soul speak in the softest voice,' he said.

Tahir Shah

The Frog Prince

In old times when wishing still helped one, there lived a king whose daughters were all beautiful, but the youngest was so beautiful that the sun itself, which has seen so much, was astonished whenever it shone in her face.

Close by the King's castle lay a great dark forest, and under an old lime tree in the forest was a well, and when the day was very warm, the King's child went out into the forest and sat down by the side of the cool fountain, and when she was dull she took a golden ball, and threw it up on high and caught it, and this ball was her favourite plaything.

Now it so happened that on one occasion the princess's golden ball did not fall into the little hand which she was holding up for it, but on to the ground beyond, and rolled straight into the water. The King's daughter followed it with her eyes, but it vanished, and the well was deep, so deep that the bottom could not be seen.

On this she began to cry, and cried louder and louder, and could not be comforted. And as she thus lamented, someone said to her, 'What ails you, King's daughter? You weep so that even a stone would show pity.'

She looked round to the side from whence the voice came, and saw a frog stretching forth its thick, ugly head from the water.

'Ah! Old water-splasher, is it you?' said she; 'I am weeping for my golden ball, which has fallen into the well.'

'Be quiet, and do not weep,' answered the frog, 'I can help you, but what will you give me if I bring your plaything up again?'

'Whatever you will have, dear frog,' said she, 'my clothes, my pearls and jewels, and even the golden crown which I am wearing.'

The frog answered, 'I do not care for your clothes, your pearls and jewels, or your golden crown, but if you will love me and let me be thy companion and playfellow, and sit by you at your little table, and eat off your little golden plate, and drink out of your little cup, and sleep in your little bed – if you wilt promise me this, I will go down below, and bring you your golden ball up again.'

'Oh, yes,' said she, 'I promise you all you wish, if you will but bring me my ball back again.' She, however, thought, 'How the silly frog does talk! He lives in the water with the other frogs and croaks, and can be no companion to any human being!'

But the frog when he had received this promise, put his head into the water and sank down, and in a short time came swimming up again with the ball in his mouth, and threw it on the grass. The King's daughter was delighted to see her pretty plaything once more, and picked it up, and ran away with it.

'Wait, wait,' said the frog, 'Take me with you. I can't run as you can.'

But what did it avail him to scream his croak, croak, after her, as loudly as he could? She did not listen to it, but ran home and soon forgot the poor frog, who was forced to go back into his well again.

The next day when she had seated herself at table with the King and all the courtiers, and was eating from her little golden plate, something came creeping splish-splash, splish-splash, up the marble staircase, and when it had got to the top, it knocked at the door and cried, 'Princess, youngest princess, open the door for me.'

She ran to see who was outside, but when she opened the door, there sat the frog in front of it. Then she slammed the door to, in great haste, sat down to dinner again, and was quite frightened.

The King saw plainly that her heart was beating violently, and said, 'My child, what are you so afraid of? Is there perchance a giant outside who wants to carry you away?'

'Ah, no,' replied she, 'it is no giant, but a disgusting frog.'

'What does the frog want with you?'

'Ah, dear father, yesterday when I was in the forest sitting by the well, playing, my golden ball fell into the water. And because I cried so, the frog brought it out again for me, and because he insisted so on it, I promised him he should be my companion, but I never thought he would be able to come out of his water! And now he is outside there, and wants to come in to me.'

In the meantime, it knocked a second time, and cried,

'Princess! Youngest princess!
Open the door for me!
Do you not know what you said to me
Yesterday by the cool waters of the fountain?
Princess, youngest princess!
Open the door for me!'

Then said the King, 'That which you have promised must you perform. Go and let him in.'

She went and opened the door, and the frog hopped in and followed her, step by step, to her chair. There, he sat still and cried, 'Lift me up beside you.'

She delayed until at last, the King commanded her to do it. When the frog was once on the chair he wanted to be on the table, and when he was on the table he said, 'Now, push your little golden plate nearer to me that we may eat together.'

She did this, but it was easy to see that she did not do it willingly. The frog enjoyed what he ate, but almost every mouthful she took choked her.

At length he said, 'I have eaten and am satisfied; now I am tired, carry me into your little room and make your little silken bed ready, and we will both lie down and go to sleep.'

The King's daughter began to cry, for she was afraid of the cold frog which she did not like to touch, and which was now to sleep in her pretty, clean little bed.

But the King grew angry and said, 'He who helped you when you were in trouble ought not afterwards to be despised by you.'

So she took hold of the frog with two fingers, carried him upstairs, and put him in a corner. But when she was in bed he crept to her and said, 'I am tired, I want to sleep as well as you, lift me up or I will tell your father.'

Then she was terribly angry, and took him up and threw him with all her might against the wall.

'Now, you will be quiet, odious frog,' said she.

But when he fell down, he was no frog – but a king's son with beautiful kind eyes. He by her father's will was now her dear companion and husband. Then he told her how he had been bewitched by a wicked witch, and how no one could have delivered him from the well but herself, and that tomorrow they would go together into his kingdom. Then they went to sleep, and next morning when the sun awoke them, a carriage came driving up with eight white horses, which had white ostrich feathers on their heads, and were harnessed with golden chains, and behind stood the young King's servant faithful Henry. Faithful Henry had been so unhappy when his master was changed into a frog that he had caused three iron bands to be laid round his heart, lest it should burst with grief and sadness. The carriage was to conduct the young King into his kingdom. Faithful Henry helped them both in, and placed himself behind again, and was full of joy because of this deliverance. And when they had driven a part of the way, the King's son heard a cracking behind him as if something had broken.

So he turned round and cried, 'Henry, the carriage is breaking.'

'No, master, it is not the carriage. It is a band from my heart, which was put there in my great pain when you were a frog and imprisoned in the well.'

Again and once again while they were on their way something cracked, and each time the King's son thought the carriage was breaking; but it was only the bands which were springing from the heart of faithful Henry because his master was set free and was happy.

From: Household Tales by the Brothers Grimm

The Buffalo & the Fieldmouse

ONCE UPON A time, when the Fieldmouse was out gathering wild beans for the winter, his neighbour, the Buffalo, came down to graze in the meadow. This the little Mouse did not like, for he knew that the other would mow down all the long grass with his prickly tongue, and there would be no place in which to hide. He made up his mind to offer battle like a man.

'Ho, Friend Buffalo, I challenge you to a fight!' he exclaimed in a small, squeaking voice.

The Buffalo paid no attention, no doubt thinking it only a joke. The Mouse angrily repeated the challenge, and still his enemy went on quietly grazing. Then the little Mouse laughed with contempt as he offered his defiance.

The Buffalo at last looked at him and replied carelessly: 'You had better keep still, little one, or I shall come over there and step on you, and there will be nothing left!'

'You can't do it!' replied the Mouse.

'I tell you to keep still,' insisted the Buffalo, who was getting angry. 'If you speak to me again, I shall certainly come and put an end to you!'

'I dare you to do it!' said the Mouse, provoking him.

Thereupon the other rushed upon him. He trampled the grass clumsily and tore up the earth with his front hoofs. When he had ended, he looked for the Mouse, but he could not see him anywhere.

'I told you I would step on you, and there would be nothing left!' he muttered.

Just then he felt a scratching inside his right ear. He shook his head as hard as he could and twitched his ears back and forth. The gnawing went deeper and deeper until he was half wild with the pain. He pawed with his hoofs and tore up the sod with his horns. Bellowing madly, he ran as fast as he could, first straight forward and then in circles, but at last he stopped and stood trembling.

Then the Mouse jumped out of his ear, and said: 'Will you own now that I am master?'

'No!' bellowed the Buffalo, and again he started toward the Mouse, as if to trample him under his feet. The little fellow was nowhere to be seen, but in a minute the Buffalo felt him in the other ear. Once more he became wild with pain, and ran here and there over the prairie, at times leaping high in the air. At last, he fell to the ground and lay quite still.

The Mouse came out of his ear and stood proudly upon his dead body. 'Eho!' said he, 'I have killed the greatest of all beasts. This will show to all that I am master!'

Standing upon the body of the dead Buffalo, he called loudly for a knife with which to dress his game.

In another part of the meadow, Red Fox, very hungry, was hunting mice for his breakfast. He saw one and jumped upon him with all four feet, but the little Mouse got away, and he was dreadfully disappointed.

All at once he thought he heard a distant call: 'Bring a knife! Bring a knife!'

When the second call came, Red Fox started in the direction of the sound. At the first knoll he stopped and listened, but hearing nothing more, he was about to go back. Just then he heard the call plainly, but in a very thin voice, 'Bring a knife!'

Red Fox immediately set out again and ran as fast as he could.

By and by he came upon the huge body of the Buffalo lying upon the ground. The little Mouse still stood upon the body.

'I want you to dress this Buffalo for me and I will give you some of the meat,' commanded the Mouse.

'Thank you, my friend, I shall be glad to do this for you,' he replied, politely.

The Fox dressed the Buffalo, while the Mouse sat upon a mound nearby, looking on and giving his orders.

'You must cut the meat into small pieces,' he said to the Fox.

When the Fox had finished his work, the Mouse paid him with a small piece of liver. He swallowed it quickly and smacked his lips.

'Please, may I have another piece?' he asked quite humbly.

'Why, I gave you a very large piece! How greedy you are!' exclaimed the Mouse. 'You may have some of the blood clots,' he sneered. So, the poor Fox took the blood clots and even licked off the grass. He was really very hungry.

'Please may I take home a piece of the meat?' he begged. 'I have six little folks at home, and there is nothing for them to eat.'

'You can take the four feet of the Buffalo. That ought to be enough for all of you!'

'Hi, hi! Thank you, thank you!' said the Fox. 'But, Mouse, I have a wife also, and we have had bad luck in hunting. We are almost starved. Can't you spare me a little more?'

'Why,' declared the Mouse, 'I have already overpaid you for the little work you have done. However, you can take the head, too!'

Thereupon the Fox jumped upon the Mouse, who gave one faint squeak and disappeared.

If you are proud and selfish, you will lose all in the end.

From: Wigwam Evenings Sioux Folk Tales Retold

Why the Sun & the Moon Live in the Sky

MANY YEARS AGO, the sun and water were great friends, and both lived on the earth together. The sun very often used to visit the water, but the water never returned his visits. At last the sun asked the water why it was that he never came to see him in his house; the water replied that the sun's house was not big enough, and that if he came with his people, he would drive the sun out.

He then said, 'If you wish me to visit you, you must build a very large compound; but I warn you that it will have to be a tremendous place, as my people are very numerous, and take up a lot of room.'

The sun promised to build a very big compound, and soon afterwards he returned home to his wife, the moon, who greeted him with a broad smile when he opened the door. The sun told the moon what he had promised the water, and the next day commenced building a huge compound in which to entertain his friend.

When it was completed, he asked the water to come and visit him the next day.

When the water arrived, he called out to the sun, and asked him whether it would be safe for him to enter, and the sun answered, 'Yes, come in, my friend.'

The water then began to flow in, accompanied by the fish and all the water animals.

Very soon the water was knee-deep, so he asked the sun if it was still safe, and the sun again said,

'Yes,' so more water came in.

When the water was level with the top of a man's head, the water said to the sun,

'Do you want more of my people to come?' and the sun and moon both answered, 'Yes,' not knowing any better, so the water flowed on, until the sun and moon had to perch themselves on the top of the roof.

Again the water addressed the sun, but receiving the same answer, and more of his people rushing in, the water very soon overflowed the top of the roof, and the sun and moon were forced to go up into the sky, where they have remained ever since.

From: Folk Stories from Southern Nigeria

The Little Settlement

THERE WAS A strong farmer one time, and he was the boastfullest man in all Ireland. He had a tidy, comfortable place, sure enough, but to hear him speaking, you'd be thinking his house was built of silver and thatched with the purest gold.

Herself was a very different sort of a person, kindly and simple-hearted; she took no pleasure in making out she had more property and grandeur than another body; and she was neither envious, uncharitable, nor a clash.

The two had but one child, a daughter, and she was their whole delight. Bride was a beautiful girl with a countenance on her would charm a king from his golden throne to be walking the bogs with herself. The boys were flocking after her by the score, and she had but to raise her hand to draw any one of them to her side. But, being a seemly, well-reared lass, she took her diversion without any consideration of marriage at all – well satisfied her father would be making a fitting settlement for her when the time came.

The youth of the world will always be playing themselves and chatting together, all the while them that have right wit and a good upbringing do leave their settlement in the hands of the parents have the best understanding for the same.

'I'm thinking,' says himself one evening, 'that it's old and stiff I am growing. It might be a powerful advantage to take a son-in-law into the place; that way I'd get sitting in peace by the hearth, and he out in the fields attending to the management of all.'

'Bride is full young to be joining the world,' says his wife. 'But I will not be putting any hindrance in the way of it, for maybe it's better contented she'd be to have a fine man of her own, foreby to be looking on an old pair like ourselves, and we dozing by the fire of an evening.'

'I'll be making a little settlement for her, surely,' says himself.

The next day, he gave out through the country that Bride was to be married. What with the little handful of money, the fine farm of land and the looks of the girl, the suitors were coming in plenty. There were strong farmers, small farmers, tradesmen and dealers; a cow doctor, a blacksmith, and evenly a man that travelled in tea. Himself was disgusted with all; he put out the farmers and dealers very civil and stiff, but the tea man he stoned down the road for a couple of miles.

The next suitor to come was a beautiful young lad the name of Shan Alec. He was a tasty worker, and he had the best of good money was left him by his da. Now if you were to seek all Ireland ten times through, I'll go bail you wouldn't be finding a more suitable match nor Shan Alec and Bride. The girl and her mother were fair wild with delight, but they got an odious disappointment for didn't himself run the poor boy out of the house.

'I'm surprised at you,' says the wife. 'Why couldn't you have wit and give that decent lad an honourable reception?'

'Is it to give my daughter to yon country coley?' says he. 'And I the warmest man in these parts.'

'A better match for her like isn't walking this earth,' says the wife.

'Hold your whisht, woman,' says he. 'I'd sooner let the devil have her than see her join the world with Shan Alec.'

'What is on you at all to be speaking such foolishness?' asks herself.

'I'd have you to know,' says he, 'that I'll have a gentleman for my son-in-law and no common person at all.'

'It is the raving of prosperity is on you,' says she. 'And that is the worst madness out.'

'Speak easy,' says he, 'or maybe I'll correct you with the pot stick.'

With that, she allowed he be to be gone daft entirely, or he'd never have such an unseemly thought as to raise his hand to a woman.

'Hold your whisht,' he answers. 'Surely 'tis both hand and foot I'll be giving you unless you quit tongueing.'

Not a long afterwards, a splendid gentleman came to the house, and he riding on a horse.

'I have heard tell,' says he to the farmer, 'that you are seeking a suitable settlement for your daughter.'

'If your honour wants a wife,' says himself. 'Let you be stepping in, for it's maybe in this house you'll find her.'

With that, the gentleman got down off his horse, and it was an honourable reception they made him. Evenly herself was content to remember the scorn put on poor Shan Alec, when she seen the magnificent suitor was come.

The gentleman had a smile on his face when he heard all the boasts of the farmer.

'My good man,' says he, 'I think scorn on your money and land, for I'd have you to know that I am a King in my own place. But that girl sitting by the hearth has a lovely white countenance on her, and her heart I am seeking for love of the same.'

'Oh mother,' says Bride in a whisper, 'will you send him away?'

'Is it raving you are?' asks herself.

'I'd go through fire and water for my poor Shan Alec!' says Bride.

'Will you hold your whisht,' says her mother. 'That is no right talk for a well-reared girl.'

The farmer and the gentleman made their agreement and opened the bottle of whiskey. There was to be a nice little feast for to celebrate the settlement, and the cloth was set in the parlour on account of the grandeur of the suitor and he not used to a kitchen at all.

When the supper was served, didn't the servant girl call the mistress out to the kitchen.

'Oh mam,' says she. 'I couldn't get word with you in private before. Let you hunt that lad from the place.'

'And why, might I ask?' says herself.

'Sure, how would he be a right gentleman and he having a foot on him like a horse?' says the girl.

With that the mistress began to lament and to groan. 'What'll I do! What'll I do, and I scared useless with dread?'

'I'll go in and impeach him,' says the servant girl.

In she went to the parlour. 'Quit off out of this,' says she. 'We'll have no horse feet in this place.'

The master got up to run her from the room.

'Look under the table at your lovely gentleman's foot!' says she.

The farmer done as she bid, but he was that set in his own conceit he just answers: 'What harm is in a reel foot? It's no ornament surely, but that's all there is to it.'

'Many's the reel foot I've laid eyes on,' she says. 'But yon is the hoof of a horse.'

'It's truth you are speaking,' says the gentleman. 'I am the devil and no person less.'

'Quit off from here,' says the servant. 'A decent girl, like us two, need never be fearing your like. I'd hit you a skelp with the pot stick as soon as I'd stand on a worm.'

'You can't put me out,' says the devil. 'For the man of the house has me promised his daughter.'

'There is no person living,' says Bride, 'might have power on the soul of another. If my sins don't deliver me into your hand the word of my da is no use.'

'Then I'll be taking himself,' says the devil, making ready to go.

'You may wait till he's dead,' cries the woman of the house. 'He made you no offer of his bones and his flesh.'

'The tongues of three women would argue the devil to death,' says he, and away with him in a grey puff of smoke. The man and woman of the house began for to pray.

But says Bride to the servant: 'Let you slip off to Shan Alec and bid him come up – for it's maybe an honourable reception is waiting him here.'

From: Folk Tales of Breffny

Fatima's Deliverance

My brother Mustapha and my sister Fatima were almost of the same age; the former was at most but two years older. They loved each other fervently, and did in concert, all that could lighten, for our suffering father, the burden of his old age.

On Fatima's seventeenth birthday, my brother prepared a festival. He invited all her companions and set before them a choice banquet in the gardens of our father, and, towards evening, proposed to them to take a little sail upon the sea, in a boat which he had hired, and adorned in grand style. Fatima and her companions agreed with joy, for the evening was fine, and the city, particularly when viewed by evening from the sea, promised a magnificent prospect. The girls, however, were so well pleased upon the bark, that they continually entreated my brother to go farther out upon the sea. Mustapha, however, yielded reluctantly, because a Pirate had been seen, for several days back, in that vicinity.

Not far from the city, a promontory projected into the sea; thither the maidens were anxious to go, in order to see the sun sink into the water. Having rowed thither, they beheld a boat occupied by armed men. Anticipating no good, my brother commanded the oarsmen to turn the vessel, and make for land. His apprehensions seemed, indeed, to be confirmed, for the boat quickly approached that of my brother, and getting ahead of it, (for it had more rowers,) ran between it and the land. The young girls, moreover, when they knew the danger to which they were exposed, sprang up with cries and lamentations: in vain Mustapha sought to quiet them, in vain enjoined upon them to be still, lest their running to and fro should upset the vessel. It was of no avail; and when, in consequence of the proximity of the other boat, all ran upon the further side, it was upset.

Meanwhile, they had observed from the land the approach of the strange boat, and, inasmuch as, for some time back, they had been in anxiety on account of pirates, their suspicions were excited, and several boats put off from the land to their assistance: but they only came in time to pick up the drowning. In the confusion, the hostile boat escaped. In both barks, however, which had taken in those who were preserved, they were uncertain whether all had been saved. They approached each other, and alas! found that my sister and one of her companions were missing; at the same time, in their number a stranger was discovered, who was known to none. In answer to Mustapha's threats, he confessed that he belonged to the hostile ship, which was lying at anchor two miles to the eastward, and that his companions had left him behind in their hasty flight, while he was engaged in assisting to pick up the maidens; moreover, he said he had seen two taken on board their boat.

The grief of my old father was without bounds, but Mustapha also was afflicted unto death, for not only had his beloved sister been lost, and did he accuse himself of having been the cause of her misfortune, but, also, her companion who had shared it with her, had been promised to him by her parents as his wife; still had he not dared to avow it to our father, because her family was poor, and of low descent. My father, however, was a stern man; as soon as his sorrow had subsided a little, he called Mustapha before him, and thus spoke to him: –

'Your folly has deprived me of the consolation of my old age, and the joy of my eyes. Go! I banish you forever from my sight! I curse you and your offspring – and only when you shall restore to me my Fatima, shall your head be entirely free from a father's execrations!'

This my poor brother had not expected; already, before this, he had determined to go in search of his sister and her friend, after having asked the blessing of his father upon his efforts, and now that father had sent him forth into the world, laden with his curse. As, however, his former grief had bowed him down, so this consummation of misfortune, which he had not deserved, tended to steel his mind. He went to the imprisoned pirate, and, demanding whither the ship was bound, learned that she carried on a trade in slaves, and usually had a great sale thereof in Balsora.

On his return to the house, in order to prepare for his journey, the anger of his father seemed to have subsided a little, for he sent him a purse full of gold, to support him during his travels. Mustapha, thereupon, in tears took leave of the parents of Zoraida, (for so his affianced was called,) and set out upon the route to Balsora.

Mustapha travelled by land, because from our little city there was no ship that went direct to Balsora. He was obliged, therefore, to use all expedition, in order not to arrive too long after the sea-robbers. Having a good horse and no luggage, he hoped to reach this city by the end of the sixth day. On the evening of the fourth, however, as he was riding all alone upon his way, three men came suddenly upon him. Having observed that they were well-armed and powerful men, and sought his money and his horse, rather than his life, he cried out that he would yield himself to them. They dismounted and tied his feet together under his horse; then they placed him in their midst, and, without a word spoken, trotted quickly away with him; one of them having seized his bridle.

Mustapha gave himself up to a feeling of gloomy despair; the curse of his father seemed already to be undergoing its accomplishment on the unfortunate one, and how could he hope to save his sister and Zoraida, should he, robbed of all his means, even be able to devote his poor life to their deliverance? Mustapha and his silent companions might have ridden about an hour when they entered a little valley. The vale was enclosed by lofty trees; a soft, dark-green turf, and a stream which ran swiftly through its midst, invited to repose. In this place were pitched from fifteen to twenty tents, to the stakes of which were fastened camels and fine horses: from one of these tents distinctly sounded the melody of a guitar, blended with two fine manly voices. It seemed to my brother as if people who had chosen so blithesome a resting-place, could have no evil intentions towards himself; and accordingly, without apprehension, he obeyed the summons of his conductors, who had unbound his feet, and made signs to him to follow. They led him into a tent which was larger than the rest, and on the inside was magnificently fitted up. Splendid cushions embroidered with gold, woven carpets, gilded censers, would elsewhere have bespoken opulence and respectability, but here seemed only the booty of a robber band. Upon one of the cushions an old and small-sized man was reclining: his countenance was ugly; a dark-brown and shining skin, a disgusting expression around his eyes, and a mouth of malicious cunning, combined to render his whole appearance odious. Although this man sought to put on a commanding air, still Mustapha soon perceived that not for him was the tent so richly adorned, and the conversation of his conductors seemed to confirm him in his opinion.

'Where is the Mighty?' inquired they of the little man.

'He is out upon a short hunt,' was the answer; 'but he has commissioned me to attend to his affairs.'

'That has he not wisely done,' rejoined one of the robbers; 'for it must soon be determined whether this dog is to die or be ransomed, and that the Mighty knows better than you.'

Being very sensitive in all that related to his usurped dignity, the little man, raising himself, stretched forward in order to reach the other's ear with the extremity of his hand, for he seemed desirous of revenging himself by a blow; but when he saw that his attempt was fruitless, he set about abusing him (and indeed the others did not remain much in his debt) to such a degree that the tent resounded with their strife. Thereupon, of a sudden, the tent door opened, and in walked a tall, stately man, young and handsome as a Persian prince. His garments and weapons, with the exception of a richly mounted poniard and gleaming sabre, were plain and simple; his serious eye, however, and his whole appearance, demanded respect without exciting fear.

'Who is it that dares to engage in strife within my tent?' exclaimed he, as they started back aghast. For a long time, deep stillness prevailed, till at last one of those who had captured Mustapha related to him how it had begun. Thereupon, the countenance of 'the Mighty,' as they had called him, seemed to grow red with passion.

'When would I have placed thee, Hassan, over my concerns?' he cried, in frightful accents, to the little man. The latter, in his fear, shrunk until he seemed even smaller than before, and crept towards the door of the tent. One step of the Mighty was sufficient to send him through the entrance with a long singular bound. As soon as the little man had vanished, the three led Mustapha before the master of the tent, who had meanwhile reclined upon the cushion.

'Here bring we you him, whom you commanded us to take.'

He regarded the prisoner for some time, and then said, 'Bashaw of Sulieika, your own conscience will tell you why you stand before Orbasan.'

When my brother heard this, he bowed low and answered: 'My lord, you appear to labour under a mistake; I am a poor unfortunate, not the Bashaw whom you seek.'

At this all were amazed; the master of the tent, however, said: 'Dissimulation can help you little, for I will summon the people who know you well.'

He commanded them to bring in Zuleima. An old woman was led into the tent, who, on being asked whether in my brother she recognised the Bashaw of Sulieika, answered:

'Yes, verily! And I swear by the grave of the Prophet, it is the Bashaw, and no other!'

'See you, wretch, that your dissimulation has become as water?' cried out the Mighty in a furious tone. 'You are too pitiful for me to stain my good dagger with your blood, but tomorrow, when the sun is up, will I bind you to the tail of my horse, and gallop with you through the woods, until they separate behind the hills of Sulieika!'

Then sank my poor brother's courage within him. 'It is my cruel father's curse that urges me to an ignominious death,' exclaimed he, weeping; 'and you, too, art lost, sweet sister, and you, Zoraida!'

'Your dissimulation helps you not,' said one of the robbers, as he bound his hands behind his back.

'Come, out of the tent with you! For the Mighty is biting his lips and feeling for his dagger. If you would live another night, bestir yourself!'

Just as the robbers were leading my brother from the tent, they met three of their companions, who were also pushing a captive before them. They entered with him.

'Here bring we the Bashaw, as you have commanded,' said they, conducting the prisoner before the cushion of the Mighty. While they were so doing, my brother had an opportunity of examining him, and was struck with surprise at the remarkable resemblance which this man bore to himself; the only difference being that he was of more gloomy aspect, and had a black beard. The Mighty seemed much astonished at the resemblance of the two captives.

'Which of you is the right one?' he asked, looking alternately at Mustapha and the other.

'If you meanest the Bashaw of Sulieika,' answered the latter in a haughty tone, 'I am he!'

The Mighty regarded him for a long time with his grave, terrible eye, and then silently motioned to them to lead him off. This having been done, he approached my brother, severed his bonds with his dagger, and invited him by signs to sit upon the cushion beside him.

'It grieves me, stranger,' he said, 'that I took you for this villain. It has happened, however, by some mysterious interposition of Providence, which placed you in the hands of my companions at the very hour in which the destruction of this wretch was ordained.'

Mustapha, thereupon, entreated him only for permission to pursue his journey immediately, for this delay might cost him much. The Mighty asked what business it could be that required such haste, and, when Mustapha had told him all, he persuaded him to spend that night in his tent and allow his horse some rest; and promised the next morning to show him a route which would bring him to Balsora in a day and a half. My brother consented, was sumptuously entertained, and slept soundly till morning in the robber's tent.

Upon awaking, he found himself all alone in the tent, but, before the entrance, heard several voices in conversation, which seemed to belong to the swarthy little man and the bandit chief. He listened awhile, and to his horror heard the little man eagerly urging the other to slay the stranger, since, if he were let go, he could betray them all. Mustapha immediately perceived that the little man hated him for having been the cause of his rough treatment the day before.

The Mighty seemed to be reflecting a moment. 'No,' said he; 'he is my guest, and the laws of hospitality are with me sacred: moreover, he does not look like one that would betray us.'

Having thus spoken, he threw back the tent cover, and walked in. 'Peace be with you, Mustapha!' he said: 'let us taste the morning drink, and then prepare yourself for your journey.'

He offered my brother a cup of sherbet, and after they had drunk, they saddled their horses, and Mustapha mounted with a lighter heart, indeed, than when he entered the vale. They had soon turned their backs upon the tents, and took a broad path, which led into the forest. The Mighty informed my brother that this Bashaw, whom they had captured in the chase, had promised them that they should remain undisturbed within his jurisdiction; but some weeks before, he had taken one of their bravest men and had him hung, after the most terrible tortures. He had waited for him a long time, and today he must die. Mustapha ventured not to say a word in opposition, for he was glad to have escaped himself with a whole skin.

At the entrance of the forest, the Mighty checked his horse, showed Mustapha the way, and gave him his hand with these words: 'Mustapha, you became in a strange way the guest of the robber Orbasan. I will not ask you not to betray what you have seen and heard. You have unjustly endured the pains of death, and I owe you a recompense. Take this dagger as a remembrance, and when you have need of help, send it to me, and I will hasten to your assistance. This purse you will perhaps need upon your journey.'

My brother thanked him for his generosity; he took the dagger but refused the purse. Orbasan, however, pressed once again his hand, let the money fall to the ground, and galloped with the speed of the wind into the forest. Mustapha, seeing that he could not overtake him, dismounted to secure the purse, and was astonished at the great magnanimity of his host, for it contained a large sum of gold. He thanked Allah for his deliverance, commended the generous robber to his mercy, and again started, with fresh courage, upon the route to Balsora.

About the middle of the seventh day after his departure, Mustapha entered the gate of Balsora. As soon as he had arrived at a caravanserai, he inquired whether the slave market, which was held here every year, had opened; but received the startling answer, that he had come two days too late. His informer deplored his tardiness, telling him that on the last day of the market, two female slaves had arrived, of such great beauty as to attract to themselves the eyes of all the merchants.

He inquired more particularly as to their appearance, and there was no doubt in his mind, that they were the unfortunate ones of whom he was in search. Moreover, he learned that the man who had purchased them both was called Thiuli-Kos, and lived forty leagues from Balsora, an illustrious and wealthy, but quite old man, who had been in his early years Capudan-Bashaw of the Sultan, but had now settled down into private life with the riches he had acquired.

Mustapha was, at first, on the point of remounting his horse with all possible speed, in order to overtake

Thiuli-Kos, who could scarcely have had a day's start; but when he reflected that, as a single man, he could not prevail against the powerful traveller, much less rescue from him his prey, he set about reflecting for another plan, and soon hit upon one. His resemblance to the Bashaw of Sulieika, which had almost been fatal to him, suggested to him the thought of going to the house of Thiuli-Kos under this name, and, in that way, making an attempt for the deliverance of the two unfortunate maidens. Accordingly, he hired attendants and horses, in which the money of Orbasan opportunely came to his assistance, furnished himself and his servants with splendid garments, and set out in the direction of Thiuli's castle. After five days, he arrived in its vicinity. It was situated in a beautiful plain, and was surrounded on all sides by lofty walls, which were but slightly overtopped by the structure itself. When Mustapha had arrived quite near, he dyed his hair and beard black, and stained his face with the juice of a plant which gave it a brownish colour, exactly similar to that of the Bashaw. From this place, he sent forward one of his attendants to the castle, and bade him ask a night's lodging, in the name of the Bashaw of Sulieika. The servant soon returned in company with four finely attired slaves, who took Mustapha's horse by the bridle, and led him into the courtyard. There they assisted him to dismount, and four others escorted him up a wide marble staircase into the presence of Thiuli.

The latter personage, an old, robust man, received my brother respectfully, and had set before him the best that his castle could afford. After the meal, Mustapha gradually turned the conversation upon the new slaves; whereupon,

Thiuli praised their beauty, but expressed regret because they were so sorrowful; nevertheless, he believed that would go over after a time. My brother was much delighted at his reception, and, with hope beating high in his bosom, lay down to rest.

He might, perhaps, have been sleeping an hour, when he was awakened by the rays of a lamp, which fell dazzlingly upon his eyes. When he had raised himself up, he believed himself dreaming, for there before him stood the very same little, swarthy fellow of Orbasan's tent, a lamp in his hand, his wide mouth distended with a disgusting laugh. Mustapha pinched himself in the arm, and pulled his nose in order to see if he were really awake, but the figure remained as before.

'What do you wish by my bed?' exclaimed Mustapha, recovering from his amazement.

'Do not disquiet yourself so much, my friend,' answered the little man. 'I made a good guess as to the motive that brought you hither. Although your worthy countenance was still well remembered by me, nevertheless, had I not with my own hand assisted to hang the Bashaw, you might, perhaps, have deceived even me. Now, however, I am here to propose a question.'

'First of all, tell me why you came hither,' interrupted Mustapha, full of resentment at finding himself detected.

'That I will explain to you,' rejoined the other: 'I could not put up with the Mighty any longer, and therefore ran away; but you, Mustapha, were properly the cause of our quarrel, and so you must give me your sister to wife, and I will help you in your flight; give her not, and I will go to my new master, and tell him something of our new Bashaw.'

Mustapha was beside himself with fear and anger; at the very moment when he thought he had arrived at the happy accomplishment of his wishes, must this wretch come, and frustrate them all! It was the only way to carry his plan into execution – he must slay the little monster: with one bound, he sprang from the bed upon him; but the other, who might perhaps have anticipated something of the kind, let the lamp fall, which was immediately extinguished, and rushed forth in the dark, crying vehemently for help.

Now was the time for decisive action; the maids he was obliged, for the moment, to abandon, and attend only to his own safety: accordingly, he approached the window, to see if he could not spring from it. It was a tolerable distance from the ground, and on the other side stood a lofty wall, which he would have to surmount. Reflecting, he stood by the window until he heard many voices approaching his chamber: already were they at the door, when seizing desperately his dagger, and garments, he let himself down from the window. The fall was hard, but he felt that no bone was broken; immediately he sprang up and ran to the wall which surrounded the court. This, to the astonishment of his pursuers, he mounted, and soon found himself at liberty. He ran on until he came to a little forest, where he sank down exhausted. Here he reflected on what was to be done; his horses and attendants he was obliged to leave behind, but the money, which he had placed in his girdle, he had saved.

His inventive genius, however, soon pointed him to another means of deliverance. He walked through the wood until he arrived at a village, where for a small sum he purchased a horse, with the help of which, in a short time, he reached a city. There he inquired for a physician, and was directed to an old, experienced man. On this one he prevailed, by a few gold pieces, to furnish him with a medicine to produce a death-like sleep, which, by means of another, might be instantaneously removed. Having obtained this, he purchased a long false beard, a black gown, and various boxes and retorts, so that he could readily pass for a travelling physician; these articles he placed upon an ass and rode back to the castle of Thiuli-Kos. He was certain, this time, of not being recognised, for the beard disfigured him so that he scarcely knew himself.

Arrived in the vicinity of the castle, he announced himself as the physician Chakamankabudibaba, and matters turned out as he had expected. The splendour of the name procured him extraordinary favour with the old fool, who invited him to table.

Chakamankabudibaba appeared before Thiuli, and, having conversed with him scarcely an hour, the old man resolved that all his female slaves should submit to the examination of the wise physician. The latter could scarcely conceal his joy at the idea of once more beholding his beloved sister, and with palpitating heart followed Thiuli, who conducted him to his seraglio. They reached an unoccupied room, which was beautifully furnished.

'Chambaba, or whatever you may be called, my good physician,' said Thiuli-Kos, 'look once at that hole in the wall; thence shall each of my slaves stretch forth her arm, and you can feel whether the pulse betoken sickness or health.'

Answer as he might, Mustapha could not arrange it so that he might see them; nevertheless, Thiuli agreed to tell him, each time, the usual health of the one he was examining. Thiuli drew forth a long list from his girdle, and began, with loud voice, to call out, one by one, the names of his slaves; whereupon, each time, a hand came forth from the wall, and the physician felt the pulse. Six had been read off, and declared entirely well, when Thiuli, for the seventh called Fatima, and a small hand slipped forth from the wall. Trembling with joy, Mustapha grasped it, and with an important air pronounced her seriously ill. Thiuli became very anxious and commanded his wise Chakamankabudibaba straightway to prescribe some medicine for her.

The physician left the room, and wrote a little scroll: 'Fatima, I will preserve you, if you can make up your mind to take a draught, which for two days will make you dead; nevertheless, I possess the means of restoring you to life. If you will, then only return answer that this liquid has been of no assistance, and it will be to me a token that you agree.'

In a moment. he returned to the room, where Thiuli had remained. He brought with him an innocent drink, felt the pulse of the sick Fatima once more, pushed the note beneath her bracelet, and then handed her the liquid through the opening in the wall. Thiuli seemed to be in great anxiety on Fatima's account and postponed the examination of the rest to a more fitting opportunity. As he left the room with Mustapha, he addressed him in sorrowful accents: 'Chadibaba, tell me plainly, what do you think of Fatima's illness?'

My brother answered with a deep sigh: 'Ah, sir, may the Prophet give you consolation! She has a slow fever, which may, perhaps, cost her life!'

Then burned Thiuli's anger: 'What say you, cursed dog of a physician? She, for whom I gave two thousand gold pieces – shall she die like a cow? Know, if you preserve her not, I will chop off your head!'

My brother immediately saw that he had made a misstep, and again inspired Thiuli with hope. While they were yet conversing, a slave came from the seraglio to tell the physician that the drink had been of no assistance.

'Put forth all your skill, Chakamdababelda, or whatever thy name may be; I will pay you what you ask!' cried out Thiuli-Kos, well-nigh howling with sorrow at the idea of losing so much gold.

'I will give her a potion which will put her out of all danger,' answered the physician.

'Yes, yes! Give it her,' sobbed the old Thiuli.

With joyful heart, Mustapha went to bring his soporific, and having given it to the slave, and shown him how much it was necessary to take for a dose, he went to Thiuli, and, telling him he must procure some medicinal herbs from the sea, hastened through the gate. On the shore, which was not far from the castle, he removed his false garments, and cast them into the water, where they floated merrily around; concealing himself, however, in a thicket, he awaited the night, and then stole softly to the burying-place of Thiuli's castle.

Hardly an hour had Mustapha been absent, when they brought Thiuli the intelligence that his slave Fatima was in the agonies of death. He sent them to the seacoast to bring the physician back with all speed, but his messengers returned alone, with the news that the poor physician had fallen into the water, and was drowned; that they had espied his black gown floating upon the surface, and that now and then his large beard peeped forth from amid the billows. Thiuli seeing now no help, cursed himself and the whole world; plucked his beard, and dashed his head against the wall. But all this was of no use, for soon Fatima gave up the ghost in the arms of her companions. When the unfortunate man heard the news of her death, he commanded them quickly to make a coffin, for he could not tolerate a dead person in his house; and bade them bear forth the corpse to the place of burial. The carriers brought in the coffin, but quickly set it down and fled, for they heard sighs and sobs among the other piles.

Mustapha, who, concealed behind the coffins, had inspired the attendants with such terror, came forth and lighted a lamp which he had brought for that purpose. Then he drew out a vial which contained the life-restoring medicine and lifted the lid of Fatima's coffin. But what amazement seized him, when by the light of the lamp, strange features met his gaze! Neither my sister, nor Zoraida, but an entire stranger, lay in the coffin! It was some time before he could recover from this new stroke of destiny; at last, however, compassion triumphed over anger. He opened the vial and administered the liquid. She breathed – she opened her eyes – and seemed for some time to be reflecting where she was. At length, recalling all that had happened, she rose from the coffin, and threw herself, sobbing, at Mustapha's feet.

'How may I thank you, excellent being,' she exclaimed, 'for having freed me from my frightful prison?' Mustapha interrupted her expressions of gratitude by inquiring how it happened that she, and not his sister Fatima, had been preserved. The maiden looked in amazement.

'Now is my deliverance explained, which was before incomprehensible,' answered she. 'Know that in this castle I am called Fatima, and it was to me you gave your note – and the preserving-drink.'

My brother entreated her to give him intelligence of his sister and Zoraida, and learned that they were both in the castle, but, according to Thiuli's custom, had received different names; they were now called Mirza and Nurmahal. When Fatima, the rescued slave, saw that my brother was so cast down by this failure of his enterprise, she bade him take courage, and promised to show him means whereby he could still deliver both the maidens. Aroused by this thought, Mustapha was filled with new hope, and besought her to point out to him the way.

'Only five months,' said she, 'have I been Thiuli's slave; nevertheless, from the first, I have been continually meditating an escape; but for myself alone it was too difficult. In the inner court of the castle, you may have observed a fountain, which pours forth water from ten tubes; this fountain riveted my attention. I remembered in my father's house to have seen a similar one, the water of which was led up through a spacious aqueduct. In order to learn whether this fountain was constructed in the same manner, I one day praised its magnificence to Thiuli, and inquired after its architect.

'I myself built it,' answered he, 'and what you seest here is still the smallest part; for the water comes hither into it from a brook at least a thousand paces off, flowing through a vaulted aqueduct, which is as high as a man. And all this have I myself planned.'

After hearing this, I often wished only for a moment to have a man's strength, in order to roll away the stone from the side of the fountain; then could I have fled whither I would. The aqueduct now will I show to you; through it you can enter the castle by night and set them free. Only you must have at least two men with you in order to overpower the slaves which, by night, guard the seraglio.'

Thus, she spoke, and my brother Mustapha, although twice disappointed already in his expectations, once again took courage, and hoped with Allah's assistance to carry out the plan of the slave. He promised to conduct her in safety to her native land if she would assist him in entering the castle. But one thought still troubled him: namely, where he could find two or three faithful assistants. Thereupon the dagger of Orbasan occurred to him, and the promise of the robber to hasten to his assistance, when he should stand in need of help, and he therefore started with Fatima from the burying-ground to seek the chieftain.

In the same city where he had converted himself into a physician, with his last money he purchased a horse, and procured lodgings for Fatima with a poor woman in the suburbs. He, however, hastened towards the mountain where he had first met Orbasan, and reached it in three days. He soon found the tent, and unexpectedly walked in before the chieftain, who welcomed him with friendly courtesy.

He related to him his unsuccessful attempts, whereupon the grave Orbasan could not restrain himself from laughing a little now and then, particularly when he announced himself as the physician Chakamankabudibaba. At the treachery of the little man, however, he was furious; and swore, if he could find him, to hang him with his own hand. He assured my brother that he was ready to assist him the moment he should be sufficiently recovered from his ride.

Accordingly, Mustapha remained that night again in the robber's tent, and with the first morning-red they set out, Orbasan taking with him three of his bravest men, well mounted and armed. They rode rapidly, and in two days arrived at the little city, where Mustapha had left the rescued Fatima. Thence they rode on with her unto the forest, from which, at a little distance, they could see Thiuli's castle; there they concealed themselves to await the night. As soon as it was dark, guided by Fatima, they proceeded softly to the brook, where the aqueduct commenced, and soon found it.

There they left Fatima and a servant with the horses, and prepared themselves for the descent: before they started, however, Fatima once more repeated, with precision, the directions she had given; namely, that, on emerging from the fountain into the inner courtyard, they would find a tower in each corner on the right and left; that inside the sixth gate from the right tower, they would find Fatima and Zoraida guarded by two slaves. Well provided with weapons and iron implements for forcing the doors, Mustapha, Orbasan, and the two other men descended through the aqueduct; they sank, indeed, in water, up to the middle, but not the less vigorously on that account did they press forward.

In a half hour they arrived at the fountain, and immediately began to ply their tools. The wall was thick and firm but could not long resist the united strength of the four men; they soon made a breach sufficiently large to allow them to slip through without difficulty. Orbasan was the first to emerge, and then assisted the others.

Being now all in the courtyard, they examined the side of the castle which lay before them, in order to find the door which had been described. But they could not agree as to which it was, for on counting from the right tower to the left, they found one door which had been walled up, and they knew not whether Fatima had included this in her calculation.

But Orbasan was not long in making up his mind: 'My good sword will open to me this gate,' he exclaimed, advancing to the sixth, while the others followed him. They opened it and found six black slaves lying asleep upon the floor; imagining that they had missed the object of their search, they were already softly drawing back, when a figure raised itself in the corner, and in well-known accents called for help. It was the little man of the robber-encampment. But ere the slaves knew what had taken place, Orbasan sprang upon the little man, tore his girdle in two, stopped his mouth, and bound his hands behind his back; then he turned to the slaves, some of whom were already half bound by Mustapha and the two others, and assisted in completely overpowering them. They presented their daggers to the breasts of the slaves, and asked where Nurmahal and Mirza were; they confessed that they were in the next chamber. Mustapha rushed into the room, and found Fatima and

Zoraida awakened by the noise. They were not long in collecting their jewels and garments and following my brother.

Meanwhile, the two robbers proposed to Orbasan to carry off what they could find, but he forbade them, saying: 'It shall never be told of Orbasan that he enters houses by night to steal gold.' Mustapha, and those he had preserved, quickly stepped into the aqueduct, whither Orbasan promised to follow them immediately. As soon as they had departed, the chieftain and one of the robbers led forth the little man into the courtyard; there, having fastened around his neck a silken cord, which they had brought for that purpose, they hung him on the highest point of the fountain. After having thus punished the treachery of the wretch, they also entered the aqueduct, and followed Mustapha. With tears, the two maidens thanked their brave preserver, Orbasan; but he urged them in haste to their flight, for it was very probable that Thiuli-Kos would seek them in every direction.

With deep emotion, on the next day, did Mustapha and the rescued maidens part with Orbasan. Indeed, they never will forget him! Fatima, the freed slave, left us in disguise for Balsora, in order to take passage thence to her native land.

After a short and agreeable journey, my brother and his companions reached home. Delight at seeing them once more almost killed my old father; the next day after their arrival, he gave a great festival, to which all the city was invited. Before a large assemblage of relations and friends, my brother had to relate his story, and with one voice they praised him and the noble robber.

When, however, Mustapha had finished, my father arose and led Zoraida to him.

'Thus remove I,' said he with solemn voice, 'the curse from your head; take this maiden as the reward which your unwearied courage has merited. Receive my fatherly blessing: and may there never be wanting to our city, men who, in brotherly love, in prudence, and bravery, may be your equals!'

From: The Oriental Story Book

How the Speckled Hen Got Her Speckles

ONCE UPON A time, ages and ages ago, there was a little white hen. One day, she was busily engaged in scratching the soil to find worms and insects for her breakfast. As she worked, she sang over and over again her little crooning song, 'Quirrichi, quirrichi, quirrichi.'

Suddenly she noticed a tiny piece of paper lying on the ground.

'Quirrichi, quirrichi, what luck!' she said to herself. 'This must be a letter. One time when the king, the great ruler of our country, held his court in the meadow close by, many people brought him letters and laid them at his feet. Now I, too, even I, the little white hen, have a letter. I am going to carry my letter to the king.'

The next morning, the little white hen started bravely out on her long journey. She carried the letter very carefully in her little brown basket. It was a long distance to the royal palace where the king lived. The little white hen had never been so far from home in all her life.

After a while she met a friendly fox. Foxes and little white hens are not usually very good friends, you know, but this fox was a friend of the little white hen. Once upon a time, she had helped the fox to escape from a trap and the fox had never forgotten her kindness to him.

'O, little white hen, where are you going?' asked the fox.

'Quirrichi, quirrichi,' replied the little white hen, 'I am going to the royal palace to carry a letter to the king.'

'Indeed, little white hen,' said the fox, 'I should like to go with you. Give me your permission to accompany you on your journey.'

'I shall be glad to have you go with me,' said the little white hen. 'It is a very long journey to the royal palace where the king lives. Wouldn't you like me to carry you in my little brown basket?'

The fox climbed into the little brown basket. After the little white hen had gone on for some distance farther, she met a river. Once upon a time, the little white hen had done the river a kindness. He had, with great difficulty, thrown some ugly worms upon the bank and he was afraid they would crawl back in again. The little white hen had eaten them for him. Always after that, the river had been her friend.

'O, little white hen, where are you going?' the river called out as soon as he saw her.

'Quirrichi, quirrichi, I am going to the royal palace to carry a letter to the king,' replied the little white hen.

'O, little white hen, may I go with you?' asked the river.

The little white hen told the river that he might go with her and asked him to ride in the little brown basket. So, the river climbed into the little brown basket.

After the little white hen had journeyed along for a time, she came to a fire. Once upon a time, when the fire had been dying, the little white hen had brought some dried grass. The grass had given the fire new life and always after that, he had been the friend of the little white hen.

'O, little white hen, where are you going?' the fire asked.

'Quirrichi, quirrichi, I am going to the royal palace to carry a letter to the king,' replied the little white hen.

'O, little white hen, may I go with you?' asked the fire. 'I have never been to the royal palace and I have never had even a peep at the king.'

The little white hen told the fire that he might go with her and asked him to climb into the little brown basket. By this time, the little brown basket was so full that, try as they might, they couldn't make room for the fire. At last, they thought of a plan. The fire changed himself into ashes and then there was room for him to get into the basket.

The little white hen journeyed on and on, and finally she arrived at the royal palace.

'Who are you and what are you carrying in your little brown basket?' asked the royal doorkeeper when he opened the door.

'I am the little white hen, and I am carrying a letter to the king,' replied the little white hen. She didn't say a word about the fox and the river and the fire which she had in her little brown basket. She was so frightened before the great royal doorkeeper of the palace that she could hardly find her voice at all.

The royal doorkeeper invited the little white hen to enter the palace and he led her to the royal throne where the king was sitting. The little white hen bowed very low before the king – so low, in fact, that it mussed up all her feathers.

'Who are you and what is your business?' asked the king in his big, deep, kingly voice.

'Quirrichi, quirrichi, I am the little white hen,' replied the little white hen in her low, frightened, little voice. 'I have come to bring my letter to your royal majesty.'

She handed the king the piece of paper which had remained all this time at the bottom of the little brown basket. There were marks of dirt upon it where the friendly fox's feet had rested. It was damp where the river had lain. It had tiny holes in it where the fire had sat after he had turned himself into hot ashes.

'What do you mean by bringing me this dirty piece of paper?' shouted the king in his biggest, deepest, gruffest voice. 'I am highly offended. I always knew that hens were stupid little creatures, but you are quite the stupidest little hen I ever saw in all my life.

'Here,' and he turned to one of the attendants standing by the throne, 'take this stupid, little white hen and throw her out into the royal poultry yard. I think we will have her for dinner tomorrow.'

The little white hen was roughly seized by the tallest royal attendant and carried down the back stairs, through the back gate, out into the royal poultry yard. She still clung to the little brown basket which she had brought with her on her long journey to the royal palace and through all the sad experiences she had met there.

When the little white hen reached the royal poultry yard, all the royal fowls flew at her. Some plucked at her rumpled white feathers. Others tried to pick out her eyes. One pulled off the cover of the little brown basket.

Out sprang the fox from the little brown basket and in the twinkling of an eye he fell upon the fowls of the royal poultry yard. Not a single fowl was left alive.

There was such a great commotion that the king, the queen, the royal attendants and all the royal servants of the palace came rushing out to see what was the matter. The fox had already taken to his heels and the little white hen lost no time in running away too. She did not, however, forget to take her little brown basket with her.

The royal household all ran after her in swift pursuit. They had almost caught her, when the river suddenly sprang out of the little brown basket and flowed between the little white hen and her royal pursuers. They couldn't get across without canoes.

While they were getting the canoes and climbing into them, the little white hen had time to run a long way. She had almost reached a thick forest where she could easily hide herself when the royal pursuers again drew near. Then, the fire which had changed itself into hot ashes jumped out of the little brown basket. It immediately became dark, so dark that the royal household could not even see each other's faces and, of course, they could not see in which direction the little white hen was running. There was nothing for them to do but to return to the royal palace and live on beef and mutton.

The fire, which had turned itself into ashes, sprang out of the little brown basket so suddenly that it scattered ashes all over the little white hen. From that day, she was always speckled where the ashes fell upon her. The chickens of the little white hen (who was now a little speckled hen) were all speckled too. So were their chickens and their chickens and their chickens' chickens, even down to this very day. Whenever you see a speckled hen, you may know that she is descended from the little white hen who carried a letter to the king, and who, in her adventures, became the first speckled hen.

From: Fairy Tales from Brazil

The Old Woman & the Crooked Sixpence

An old woman was sweeping her house, and she found a crooked sixpence.

'What,' says she, 'shall I do with this sixpence? I will go to the market and buy a pig with it.'

She went; and as she was coming home, she came to a stile. Now, the pig would not go over the stile. The woman went on a little further and met a dog.

'Dog,' said she, 'bite pig. Piggy won't go over the stile, and I shan't get home tonight.'

But the dog would not bite the pig. The woman went on a little further, and she met a stick.

'Stick,' said she, 'beat dog. Dog won't bite pig, piggy won't go over stile, and I shan't get home tonight.'

But the stick would not. The woman went on a little further, and she met a fire.

'Fire,' said she, 'burn stick. Stick won't beat dog, dog won't bite pig, piggy won't go over the stile, and I shan't get home tonight.'

But the fire would not. The woman went on a little further and she met some water.

'Water,' said she, 'quench fire. Fire won't burn stick, stick won't beat dog,' etc.

But the water would not. The woman went on a little further, and she met an ox.

'Ox,' said she, 'drink water. Water won't quench fire,' etc.

But the ox would not. The woman went on again, and she met a butcher.

'Butcher,' said she, 'kill ox. Ox won't drink water,' etc.

But the butcher would not. The woman went on a little further and met a rope.

'Rope,' said she, 'hang butcher. Butcher won't kill ox,' etc.

But the rope would not. Again, the woman went on, and she met a rat.

'Rat,' said she, 'gnaw rope. Rope won't hang butcher,' etc.

But the rat would not. The woman went on a little further and met a cat.

'Cat,' said she, 'kill rat. Rat won't gnaw rope,' etc.

'Oh,' said the cat, 'I will kill the rat if you will fetch me a basin of milk from the cow over there.'

The old woman went to the cow and asked her to let her have some milk for the cat.

'No,' said the cow; 'I will let you have no milk unless you bring me a mouthful of hay from yonder stack.'

Away went the old woman to the stack and fetched the hay and gave it to the cow. Then the cow gave her some milk, and the old woman took it to the cat.

When the cat had lapped the milk, the cat began to kill the rat, the rat began to gnaw the rope, the rope began to hang the butcher, the butcher began to kill the ox, the ox began to drink the water, the water began to quench the fire, the fire began to burn the stick, the stick began to beat the dog, the dog began to bite the pig, and piggy, in a fright, jumped over the stile, and so, after all, the old woman got safe home that night.

From: Folk-lore & legends

How the Peacock Got His Beautiful Feathers

WHEN THE WORLD was young and when all the animals spoke the language of mankind, the peacock, U Klew, was but an ordinary grey-feathered bird without any pretensions to beauty. But, even in those days, he was much given to pride and vanity, and strutted about with all the majesty of royalty, just because his tuft was more erect than the tuft of other birds and because his tail was longer and was carried with more grace than the tails of any of his companions.

He was a very unaccommodating neighbour. His tail was so big and unwieldy that he could not enter the houses of the more lowly birds, so he always attended the courts of the great, and was entertained by one or other of the wealthy birds at times of festivals in the jungle. This increased his high opinion of himself and added to his self-importance. He became so haughty and overbearing that he was cordially disliked by his neighbours, who endeavoured to repay him by playing many a jest at his expense.

They used to flatter him, pretending that they held him in very high esteem, simply for the amusement of seeing him swelling his chest and hearing him boast. One day, they pretended that a great Durbar of the birds had been held to select an ambassador to carry the greetings of the jungle birds to the beautiful maiden Ka Sngi, who ruled in the Blue Realm and poured her bright light so generously on their world, and that U Klew had been chosen for this great honour.

The peacock was very elated and became more swaggering than ever, and talked of his coming visit with great boastings, saying that not only was he going as the ambassador from the birds, but he was going in his own interests as well, and that he would woo and win the royal maiden for his wife and live with her in the Blue Realm.

The birds enjoyed much secret fun at his expense, none of them dreaming that he would be foolish enough to make the attempt to fly so far, for he was such a heavy-bodied bird and had never flown higher than a treetop.

But much to the surprise of everyone, the peacock expressed his intention of starting to the Blue Realm and bade his friends goodbye, they laughing among themselves, thinking how ridiculous he was making himself, and how angry he would be when he found how he had been duped. Contrary to their expectations, however, U Klew continued his flight upwards till they lost sight of him, and they marvelled and became afraid, not knowing to what danger their jest might drive him.

Strong on the wing, U Klew soared higher and higher, never halting till he reached the sky and alighted at the palace of Ka Sngi, the most beautiful of all maidens and the most good.

Now Ka Sngi was destined to live alone in her grand palace, and her heart often yearned for companionship. When she saw that a stranger had alighted at her gates she rejoiced greatly and hastened to receive him with courtesy and welcome. When she learned the errand upon which he had come, she was still happier, for she thought, 'I shall never pine for companionship again, for this noble bird will always live with me'; and she smiled upon the world and was glad.

When U Klew left the earth and entered the realm of light and sunshine, he did not cast from him his selfish and conceited nature, but rather his selfishness and conceit grew more pronounced as his comforts and luxuries increased. Seeing the eager welcome extended to him by the beautiful maiden, he became more uplifted and exacting than ever and demanded all sorts of services at her hands; he grew surly and cross unless she was always in attendance upon him. Ka Sngi, on the other hand, was noble and generous and delighted to render kindnesses to others. She loved to shine upon the world and to see it responding to her warmth and her smiles. To her mate, U Klew, she gave unstinted attention and waited upon him with unparalleled love and devotion, which he received with cold indifference, considering that all this attention was due to his own personal greatness, rather than to the gracious and unselfish devotion of his consort.

In former times, Ka Sngi had found one of the chief outlets for her munificence in shedding her warm rays upon the earth; but after the coming of U Klew, her time became so absorbed by him that she was no longer able to leave her palace, so the earth became cold and dreary, and the birds in the jungle became cheerless, their feathers drooped, and their songs ceased. U Slap, the rain, came and pelted their cosy nests without mercy, causing their young ones to die; U Lyoh, the mist, brought his dark clouds and hung them over the rice fields so that no grain ripened; and Ka Eriong, the storm, shook the trees, destroying all the fruit, so that the birds wandered about homeless and without food.

In their great misery, they sought counsel of mankind, whom they knew to be wiser than any of the animals. By means of divinations, mankind ascertained that all these misfortunes were due to the presence of U Klew in the Blue Realm, for his selfish disposition prevented Ka Sngi from bestowing her light and her smiles upon the world as in former times; and there was no hope for prosperity until U Klew could be lured back to jungle-land.

In those days, there lived in the jungle a cunning woman whose name was Ka Sabuit. Acting on the advice of mankind, the birds invoked her aid to encompass the return of the peacock from the Blue Realm. At that time, Ka Sabuit was very destitute owing to the great famine; she had nothing to eat except some wild roots and no seed to sow in her garden except one gourdful of mustard seeds – the cheapest and most common of all seeds – and even this she was afraid to sow, lest the hungry birds should come and devour it and leave her without a grain.

When the birds came to seek counsel of her, she was very pleased, hoping that she could by some design force them to promise not to rob her garden. After they had explained to her their trouble, she undertook to bring U Klew back to the jungle within thirteen moons on two conditions: one, that the birds should refrain from picking the seeds from her garden; the other, that they should torment the animals if they came to eat her crops or to trample on her land. These appeared such easy terms that the birds readily agreed to them.

The garden of the cunning woman was in an open part of the jungle and could be seen from many of the hilltops around, and in past days the sun used to shine upon it from morning till night. Thither Ka Sabuit wended her way after the interview with the birds, and she began to dig the ground with great care and patience, bestowing much more time upon it than she had ever been known to do. Her neighbours laughed and playfully asked her if she expected a crop of precious stones to grow from her mustard seed that year that she spent so much labour upon the garden, but the elderly dame took no heed. She worked on patiently and kept her own counsel while the birds waited and watched.

She shaped her mustard bed like unto the form of a woman; this provoked the mirth of her neighbours still more and incited many questions from them, but Ka Sabuit took no heed. She worked patiently on and kept her own counsel while the birds waited and watched.

By and by the seeds sprouted and the plot of land shaped like a woman became covered with glistening green leaves, while the birds continued to watch and to keep the animals at bay, and the cunning woman watered and tended her garden, keeping her own counsel.

In time, small yellow flowers appeared on all the mustard plants, so that the plot of land shaped like a woman looked in the distance like a beautiful maiden wearing a mantle of gold that dazzled the eyes. When the neighbours saw it, they wondered at the beauty of it and admired the skill of the cunning woman; but no one could understand or guess at her reason for the strange freak and Ka Sabuit threw no light on the matter. She still patiently worked on and kept her own counsel.

Up in the Blue Realm, U Klew continued his despotic and arrogant sway, while his gentle and noble wife spared no pains to gratify his every wish. Like all pampered people who are given all their desires, the peacock became fretful and more and more difficult to please, tiring of every diversion, and ever seeking some new source of indulgence, till at last nothing seemed to satisfy him; even the splendours and magnificence of the palace of Ka Sngi began to pall.

Now and then memories of his old home and old associates came to disturb his mind, and he often wondered to himself what had been the fate of his old playmates in jungle-land. One day, he wandered forth from the precincts of the palace to view his old haunts, and as he recognised one familiar landmark after another, his eye was suddenly arrested by the sight of (as it seemed to him) a lovely maiden dressed all in gold lying asleep in a garden in the middle of the forest where he himself had once lived. At sight of her, his heart melted like water within him for the love of her. He forgot the allegiance due to his beautiful and high-born wife, Ka Sngi; he could only think of the maiden dressed all in gold, lying asleep in a jungle garden, guarded by all the birds.

After this, U Klew was reluctant to remain in the Blue Realm. His whole being yearned for the maiden he had seen lying asleep on the earth, and one day, to his wife's sorrow, he communicated his determination to return to his native land to seek the object of his new love. Ka Sngi became a sorrowful wife, for there is no pang so piercing to the heart of a constant woman as the pang inflicted by being forsaken by her husband. With all manner of inducements and persuasions and charms, she tried to prevail upon him to keep faithful to his marriage vows, but he was heartless and obdurate; and, unmindful of all ties, he took his departure. As he went away, Ka Sngi followed him, weeping, and as she wept, her tears bedewed his feathers, transforming them into all the colours of the rainbow. Some large drops falling on his long tail as he flew away were turned into brilliant-hued spots, which are called 'Ummat Ka Sngi' (the Sun's tears) by the Khasis to this day. Ka Sngi told him that they were given for a sign that wherever he might be and on whomsoever his affections might be bestowed, he would never be able to forget her, Ka Sngi, the most beautiful and the most devoted of wives.

Thus, U Klew, the peacock, came back to the jungle. The birds, when they saw his beautiful feathers, greeted him with wonder and admiration. When he informed them that he had come in quest of a lovely maiden dressed all in gold, they began to laugh, and it now became clear to them what had been the object of the cunning woman when she shaped her mustard bed like unto the shape of a woman. They invited U Klew to come and be introduced to the object of his love, and they led him forth with great ceremony to the garden of Ka Sabuit, where he beheld, not a beautiful maiden as he had imagined, but a bed of common mustard cunningly shaped. His shame and humiliation were pitiful to behold; he tried to fly back to the Blue Realm, but he was no longer able to take a long flight; so, uttering the most sad and plaintive cries, he had to resign himself to the life of the jungle for ever.

Every morning, it is said, the peacock can be seen stretching forth his neck towards the sky and flapping his wings to greet the coming of Ka Sngi; and the only happiness left to him is to spread his lovely feathers to catch the beams which she once more sheds upon the earth.

From: Folk-Tales of the Khasis

A Legend of St. Bartholomew

It is a point of faith accepted by all devout Portuguese that thirty-three baths in the sea must be taken on or before the 24th of August of every year. Although the motive may not seem to be very reasonable, still the result is of great advantage to those believers who occupy thirty-three days in taking the thirty-three baths, for otherwise the majority of them would never undergo any form of ablution.

That the demon is loose on the 24th of August is an established fact among the credulous; and were it not for the compact entered into between St. Bartholomew and said demon that all who have taken thirty-three baths during the year should be free from his talons, the list of the condemned would be much increased.

Now, there was a very powerful baron whose castle was erected on the eastern slope of the Gaviarra, overlooking the neighbouring provinces of Spain, and he had always refused to take these thirty-three baths, for he maintained that it was cowardly on the part of a man to show any fear of the demon. His castle was fully manned; the drawbridge was never left lowered; the turrets were never left unguarded; and a wide and deep ditch surrounded the whole of his estates, which had been given him by Affonso Henriques after the complete overthrow of the Saracens at Ourique, in which famous and decisive battle the baron had wrought wondrous deeds of bravery.

All round the castle were planted numerous vines, which had been brought from Burgundy by order of Count Henry, father of the first Portuguese king; and in the month of August the grapes are already well formed, but the hand of Nature has not yet painted them. Among the vines quantities of yellow melons and green watermelons were strewn over the ground, while the mottled pumpkins hung gracefully from the branches of the orange trees.

In front of the castle was an arbour, formed of box-trees, under which a lovely fountain had been constructed; and here, in the hot summer months, would wander the baron's only daughter, Alina. She was possessed of all the qualities, mental and physical, which went towards making the daughter of a feudal lord desired in marriage by all the gallants of the day; and as she was heiress to large estates, these would have been considered a sufficient prize without the said qualities. But Alina, for all this, was not happy, for she was enamoured of a handsome chief who, unfortunately, wore the distinctive almexia, which proved him to be a Moor, and, consequently, not a fit suitor for the daughter of a Christian baron.

'My father,' she would often soliloquize, 'is kind to me, and professes to be a Christian. My lover, as a follower of the Prophet, hates my father, but, as a man, he loves me. For me, he says he will do anything; yet, when I ask him to become a Christian, he answers me that he will do so if I can prevail on my father to so far conform with the Christian law as to take the thirty-three baths; and this my father will not do. What am I to do? He would rather fight the demon than obey the saint.'

One day, however, she resolved on telling her father about her courtship with the young chief, Al-Muli, and of the only condition he made, on which depended his becoming a convert to Christianity, which so infuriated the baron that, in his anger, he declared himself willing to meet the demon in mortal combat, hoping thus to free the world of him and of the necessity of taking the thirty-three baths.

This so much distressed Alina, that when, during the afternoon of the same day, Al-Muli met her in the arbour, she disclosed to him her firm resolution of entering a convent and spending the rest of her days there.

'This shall not be!' cried Al-Muli; and, seizing her round the waist, he lifted her on to his shoulder, sped through the baronial grounds and, having waded through the ditch, placed her on the albarda of his horse and galloped away.

Alina was so frightened that she could not scream, and she silently resigned herself to her fate, trusting in the honour of her lover.

The alcazar, or palace, of Al-Muli was situated on the Spanish side of the frontier; and, as they approached the principal gate, the almocadem, or captain of the guard, hurried to receive his master, who instructed him to send word to his mother that he desired of her to receive and look after Alina. This done, he assisted his bride elect to dismount, and, with a veil hiding her lovely features, she was ushered by Al-Muli's mother into a magnificently furnished room, and took a seat on a richly embroidered cushion, called an almofada.

To her future mother-in-law, she related all that referred to her conversation with her father, and how she had been brought away from his castle; and she further said that she very much feared the baron would summon all his numerous followers to rescue her.

Al-Muli's mother was a descendant of the Moors who first landed at Algeciras, and from them had descended to her that knowledge of the black art which has been peculiar to that race. She, therefore, replied that although she could count on the resistance her almogavares – or garrison soldiers – would offer to the forces of the baron, still she would do her utmost to avoid a conflict. She then proceeded to another room, in which she kept her magic mirror, and having closed the door, we must leave her consulting the oracle.

The baron was not long in discovering the absence of his daughter, and he so stormed about the place that his servants were afraid to come near him.

In a short time, however, his reason seemed to return to him, and he sat down on his old chair and gave way to grief when he saw that his Alina's cushion was vacant.

'My child – my only child and love,' sobbed the old man, 'you have left your father's castle, and gone with the accursed Moor into the hostile land of Spain. Oh, that I had been a good Christian, and looked after my daughter better! I have braved the orders of good St. Bartholomew; I would not take the thirty-three baths in the sea, and now I am wretched!'

The baron suddenly became aware of the presence of a distinguished and patriarchal looking stranger, who addressed him thus: 'You mortals only think of St. Barbara when it thunders. Now that the storm of sorrow has burst on you, you reproach yourself for not having thought of me and of my instructions. But I see that you are penitent, and if you will do as I tell you, you will regain your daughter.'

It was St. Bartholomew himself who was speaking, and the baron, for the first time in his life, shook in his shoes with fear and shame.

'Reverend saint,' at last ejaculated the baron, 'help me in this my hour of need, and I will promise you anything – and, what is more, I will keep my promises.'

'And you had better do so,' continued the saint; 'for not even Satan has dared to break his compact with me. You don't know how terrible I can be!' here the saint raised his voice to such a pitch that the castle shook. 'Only let me catch you playing false with me, and I'll – I'll – I don't know what I'll do!'

'Most reverend saint and father, you have only to command me and I will obey,' murmured the affrighted baron. 'I will indeed. Good venerable St. Bartholomew, only give me back my daughter – that is all I ask.'

'Your daughter is now in the hands of Al-Muli, her lover, who dwells in a stronger castle than yours, and who, moreover, has a mother versed in the black art. It is no good your trying to regain her by the force at your disposal; you must rely on me – only on me. Do you understand?' asked the saint.

'Yes, dear, good, noble, and venerable saint, I do understand you; but what am I to do?'

'Simply follow me, and say not a word as you go,' commanded the patriarch.

The baron did as he was told; and out from the castle the two went unseen by anyone. The baron soon perceived that he was hurrying through the air, and he was so afraid of falling that he closed his eyes. All at once, he felt that his feet were touching the ground; and, looking around him, what was his delight to find himself close to his dear daughter Alina.

'Father – dear father!' exclaimed Alina; 'how did you come here so quickly, for I have only just arrived? And how did you pass by the guards?'

The baron was going to tell her, but the saint, in a whisper, enjoined silence on this point; and the baron now noticed that the saint was invisible.

'Never mind, dear child, how I came here; it is enough that I am here,' replied her father. 'And I intend taking you home with me, dear Alina. The castle is so lonely without you;' and the old man sobbed.

At this moment Al-Muli entered the chamber, and, seeing Alina's father there, he thought there had been treachery among his guards; so, striking a gong that was near him, a number of armed men rushed in.

'How now, traitors!' said he. 'How have you been careful of your duties when you have allowed this stranger to enter unobserved?'

The soldiers protested their innocence, until at last, Al-Muli commenced to think that there must be some secret entrance into his castle.

'Search everywhere!' screamed the infuriated Moor. 'Have the guard doubled at all the entrances and send me up the captain!'

Al-Muli's instructions were carried out, and the captain reported that all was safe.

'Old man,' said the Moor, addressing the baron, 'I have you now in my power. You were the enemy of my noble race. To your blind rage my predecessors owed their downfall in Portugal. Your bitter hatred carried you to acts of vengeance. You are now in my power, but I will not harm one of your grey hairs.'

'Moor,' replied the baron, with a proud look, 'can the waters of the Manzanares and of the Guadalquivir join? No! And so cannot and may not your accursed race join with ours! Your race conquered our people, and in rising against your we did but despoil the despoiler.'

'Your logic is as baseless as your fury was wont to be,' answered the Moor. 'Though hundreds of miles separate the Manzanares from the Guadalquivir, yet do they meet in the mightier waters of the ocean. Had you said that ignorance cannot join hands with learning, you would have been nearer the mark, or that the Cross can never dim the light of the Crescent.'

These words were spoken in a haughty manner; and as Al-Muli turned round and looked upon his splendidly arrayed soldiers, who surrounded the chamber, his pride seemed justified.

'You cannot crush me more than you have done, vile Moor,' said the baron. 'You have robbed me of my daughter, not by force of arms, but stealthily, as a thief at midnight. If any spark of chivalry warmed your infidel blood, you would blush for the act you have wrought. But I fear you not, proud Moor; your warriors are no braver than your women. Dare them to move, and I will lay you at my feet.'

'Oh, my father, and you, dear Al-Muli, abandon these threats, even if you cannot be friends.'

'No, maiden,' exclaimed Al-Muli; 'I will not be bearded in my own den. Advance, guards, and take this old man to a place of safety below!'

But not a soldier moved; and when Al-Muli was about to approach them to see what was the matter with them, his scimitar dropped from his hand, and he fell on the ground.

'What charm have you brought to bear on me, bold baron,' screamed the Moor, 'that I am thus rendered powerless? Alina, if you love me, give me but that goblet full of water, for I am faint.'

Alina would have done as her lover bade her, but just then the figure of the venerable St. Bartholomew was seen with the cross in his right hand.

'Moor and infidel,' said the saint, 'you have mocked at this symbol of Christianity, and you have done grievous injury to this Christian baron; but you have been conscientious in your infidelity. Nor am I slow to recognize in your race a knowledge of the arts and sciences not yet extended to the Christian. Yet, for all this, you are but an infidel. Let me but baptize you with the water you would have drunk, and all will yet be well.'

'No, sir saint,' answered the Moor. 'When in my castle strangers thus treat me rudely, I can die, but not bend to their orders. If yonder baron is a true Christian, why has he not taken the thirty-three baths enjoined by you?'

'And if my father does take them, will you, as you did promise me,' said Alina, 'be converted to the true faith?'

'The Moor breaks not his promise. As the golondrina returns to its nest in due season, so the man of honour returns to his promise.'

Then, turning to the baron, he demanded to know if he would comply with the saint's instructions.

'Yes,' answered the baron; 'I have promised the good saint everything, and I will fulfil my promises. Al-Muli, if you love my daughter, love her faith also, and I will then have regained not only a daughter, but a son in my old age.'

'The promise of the Moor is sacred,' said Al-Muli. 'Baptize me and my household; and do you, good baron, intercede for me with the venerable saint, for I like not this lowly posture.'

'My dear Al-Muli,' sobbed Alina for joy, 'the Cross and the Crescent are thus united in the mightier ocean of love and goodwill. May the two races whom one God has made be reconciled! And tomorrow's sun must not set before we all comply with the condition imposed by St. Bartholomew.'

The saint was rejoiced with the work he had that day done and declared that the churches he liked men to construct are those built within them, where the incense offered is prayer, and the work done, love.

'As for the baths, they are but desirable auxiliaries,' said he.

From: Tales from the Lands of Nuts and Grapes

73

Simon, the Friend of Snakes

THE KING OF the Snakes lives in the ruins of a big tower between Nineveh and Babylon, and rules all the snake tribe, both on land and sea. Once the King's son, who was viceroy of the province of Diarbekir, wrote a letter to his royal father, as follows:

'Long live the King! May Heaven bestow upon you life everlasting. Amen. Be it known to you that your daughter-in-law and grandchildren were sick last summer, and the doctors advised that they must have a change of climate and must go to Mount Ararat and bathe in its pure streams, and eat its fragrant flowers, and this will immediately heal them. Consequently, I sent her and the children, with their attendants, to Mount Ararat.

'I also wrote letters to the provincial viceroys and princes to assist the Princess and her train during their sojourn in that district. But the Prince of Aderbadagan, after receiving my letter, instead of giving help to the traveling Princess, collected his troops and assaulted her and her train. The attendants of the Princess met them bravely, and there, at the foot of Mount Ararat, occurred a bloody battle, which would doubtless have resulted in the total defeat of the Princess' train, on account of the superior numbers of the enemy, if a human being, Simon the Shepherd, who was tending his flock in a neighbouring field, had not come to the assistance of our fatigued combatants.

'He took his great club, and entering the ranks of the warriors, beat and killed and pursued the assaulting brigands of the Prince of Aderbadagan, and saved the life of your daughter-in-law, who thus came safely through this perilous journey. You see, my liege, that there is good even among men. I will punish the vile Prince of Aderbadagan for his wicked conduct; but it remains for you to reward the goodness of this noble human being as you deem best and oblige your affectionate son.'

The King of the Snakes, receiving this letter, took with him a vast quantity of gold and jewels, and went to his palace in a ruined castle between Aleppo and Diarbekir. He posted his attendants on the highways to keep watch and inform him when Shepherd Simon should pass. The Shepherd was employed by dealers in livestock, who did business with Damascus and Aleppo, and was now on his way to Aleppo. As soon as he approached the palace of the Snake King, the watchers informed their sovereign, and in the twinkling of an eye the whole army of snakes stood near the highway and began to conjure. Simon the Shepherd felt a strange dizziness – the heavens above and the earth below seemed to change. He stood there bewitched, while his companions drove away. Presently he opened his eyes, and lo! He was surrounded by innumerable snakes of all sizes and colours. Upon a golden throne was sitting a snake as thick as the body of an elephant, and upon his head there was a crown of costly jewels and diamonds. One of the snakes read a paper praising the goodness of the Shepherd, his natural fondness for the snake tribe, and his gallant defence of the weak and the wronged.

'Now, noble human being,' said the King, 'here is gold for you: precious jewels and diamonds. Take as much as you like; and in addition to these, if you have a desire in your heart tell it to me and I will cause it to be satisfied.'

Simon, after filling his shepherd's bag and his pockets with gold and jewels, said: 'I wish to understand the language of all animals, reptiles and birds.'

'Let it be so,' said the King; 'but the day on which you shall tell anything of what you have seen or heard, you shall die.'

The spell was removed, the snakes vanished, and Simon the Shepherd returned to his home near the foot of Mount Ararat. On the way he heard the animals talking, and lo! They knew all the secrets of men and foretold events that would happen. Sometimes he laughed at what he heard, and sometimes he was terrified so that his hair stood erect upon his head. He entered his native village, and lo!

All the dogs, cats, chickens, and even the long-legged storks were hallooing to one another and saying: 'Simon the Shepherd has come; his bag and pockets are full of gold and jewels.'

Simon came to his house and put his treasure before his wife who, being a very curious woman, instantly asked him where and how he obtained so much wealth.

'Enjoy it, but never ask,' answered Simon.

Simon heard his dog and chickens talking in regard to the secrets of his house. Sometimes he laughed and sometimes he was angry. His wife, noticing Simon's strange conduct towards the animals, asked the reason. He refused to tell, but she begged and importuned him, weeping all the time. Finally, he could resist her entreaties no longer, and he promised to tell her everything on the following day.

That evening, he heard the dog talking to the cock, which was leading the chickens to roost, chuckling and gurgling: 'Tell me, master rooster,' said the dog, 'what is the use of your chuckling and gurgling, since our master has promised his wife tomorrow to tell her everything? He will die; people will come and kill you, shoot me, and plunder and ruin everything which belongs to our master.'

'Eh! the sooner it is ruined the better,' answered the rooster, contemptuously. 'I have a family of forty wives, who are all obedient to me; if our master was as wise as he is rich, he would not pay attention to the vain inquisitiveness of his wife; he himself would not die, and no harm would befall us or his house. But now he deserves death.'

Hearing this, Simon was advised; he seized his great club, and stood before his wife, saying: 'Wife, you must stop trying to compel me to tell you the secret; be content with what you have. Else, by Heaven, I will beat you to death!'

The woman, seeing the club brandished over her head, put an end to her inquiries, and thereafter they enjoyed a happy life.

From: The Golden Maiden & Other Folk Tales &
Fairy Stories Told in Armenia

The Ungrateful Children & the Old Father Who Went to School Again

ONCE UPON A time, there was an old man. He lived to a great age, and God gave him children whom he brought up to man's estate, and he divided all his goods amongst them.

'I will pass my remaining days among my children,' thought he.

So, the old man went to live with his eldest son, and at first the eldest son treated him properly, and did reverence to his old father.

''Tis but meet and right that we should give our father to eat and drink, and see that he has wherewithal to clothe him, and take care to patch up his things from time to time, and let him have clean new shirts on festivals,' said the eldest son.

So, they did so, and at festivals also the old father had his own glass beside him. Thus, the eldest son was a good son to his old father. But when the eldest son had been keeping his father for some time, he began to regret his hospitality, and was rough to his father, and sometimes even shouted at him. The old man no longer had his own set place in the house as heretofore, and there was none to cut up his food for him. So, the eldest son repented him that he had said he would keep his father, and he began to grudge him every morsel of bread that he put in his mouth.

The old man had nothing for it but to go to his second son. It might be better for him there or worse, but stay with his eldest son any longer he could not. So, the father went to his second son. But here the old man soon discovered that he had only exchanged wheat for straw. Whenever he began to eat, his second son and his daughter-in-law looked sour and murmured something between their teeth. The woman scolded the old man. 'We had as much as we could do before to make both ends meet,' cried she, 'and now we have old men to keep into the bargain.' The old man soon had enough of it there also, and went on to his next son.

So, one after another all four sons took their father to live with them, and he was glad to leave them all. Each of the four sons, one after the other, cast the burden of supporting him on one of the other brothers.

'It is for him to keep you, daddy!' said they; and then the other would say,

'Nay, dad, but it is as much as we can do to keep ourselves.'

Thus, between his four sons he knew not what to do. There was quite a battle among them as to which of them should not keep their old father. One had one good excuse, and another had another, and so none of them would keep him. This one had a lot of little children, and that one had a scold for a wife, and this house was too small, and that house was too poor.

'Go where you will, old man,' said they, 'only don't come to us.'

And the old man – grey, grey, grey as a dove was he – wept before his sons, and knew not whither to turn. What could he do? Entreaty was in vain. Not one of the sons would take the old man in, and yet he had to be put somewhere. Then the old man strove with them no more but let them do with him even as they would.

So, all four sons met and took counsel. Time after time they laid their heads together, and at last they agreed among themselves that the best thing the old man could do was to go to school.

'There will be a bench for him to sit upon there,' said they; 'and he can take something to eat in his knapsack.'

Then they told the old man about it; but the old man did not want to go to school. He begged his children not to send him there, and wept before them.

'Now that I cannot see the white world,' said he, 'how can I see a black book? Moreover, from my youth upward I have never learnt my letters; how shall I begin to do so now? A clerk cannot be fashioned out of an old man on the point of death!'

But there was no use talking, his children said he must go to school, and the voices of his children prevailed against his feeble old voice. So, to school he had to go.

Now there was no church in that village, so he had to go to the village beyond it to school. A forest lay along the road, and in this forest the old man met a nobleman driving along. When the old man came near to the nobleman's carriage, he stepped out of the road to let it pass, took off his hat respectfully, and then would have gone on farther. But he heard someone calling, and, looking back, saw the nobleman beckoning to him; he wanted to ask him something. The nobleman then got out of his carriage and asked the old man whither he was going. The old man took off his hat to the nobleman and told him all his misery, and the tears ran down the old man's cheeks.

'Woe is me, gracious sir! If the Lord had left me without kith and kin, I should not complain; but strange indeed is the woe that has befallen me! I have four sons, thank God, and all four have houses of their own, and yet they send their poor old father to school to learn! Was ever the like of it known before?'

So, the old man told the nobleman his whole story, and the nobleman was full of compassion for the old man.

'Well, old man,' said he, "tis no use for you to go to school, that's plain. Return home. I'll tell you what to do so that your children shall never send you to school again. Fear not, old man, weep no more, and let not your soul be troubled! God shall bless you, and all will be well. I know well what ought to be done here.'

So, the nobleman comforted the old man, and the old man began to be merry. Then the nobleman took out his purse: it was a real nobleman's purse, with a little sack in the middle of it to hold small change. Lord! What a lovely thing it was! The more he looked at it, the more the old man marvelled at it. The nobleman took this purse and began filling it full with something. When he had well filled it, he gave it to the old man.

'Take this and go home to your children,' said he, 'and when you have got home, call together all your four sons and say to them, "My dear children, long long ago, when I was younger than I am now, and knocked about in the world a bit, I made a little money. I won't spend it," I said to myself, "for one never knows what may happen.

'"So I went into a forest, my children, and dug a hole beneath an oak, and there I hid my little store of money. I did not bother much about the money afterward, because I had such good children; but when you sent me to school I came to this self-same oak, and I said to myself, 'I wonder if these few silver pieces have been waiting for their master all this time! Let us dig and see.'

'"So I dug and found them, and have brought them home to you, my children. I shall keep them till I die; but after my death consult together, and whosoever shall be found to have cherished me most and taken care of me and not grudged me a clean shirt now and then, or a crust of bread when I'm hungry, to him shall be given the greater part of my money. So now, my dear children, receive me back again, and my thanks shall be yours. You can manage it amongst you, and surely 'tis not right that I should seek a home among strangers! Which of you will be kind to your old father – for money?'"

So, the old man returned to his children with the purse in a casket, and when he came to the village with the casket under his arm, one could see at once that he had been in a good forest. When one comes home with a heavy casket under one's arm, depend upon it there's something in it! So, no sooner did the old man appear than his eldest daughter-in-law came running out to meet him and bade him welcome in God's name.

'Things don't seem to get on at all without you, dad!' cried she, 'and the house is quite dreary. Come in and rest, dad,' she went on; 'you have gone a long way and must be weary.'

Then all the brothers came together, and the old man told them what God had done for him. All their faces brightened as they looked at the casket, and they thought to themselves, 'If we keep him we shall have the money.'

Then the four brothers could not make too much of their dear old father. They took care of him, and the old man was happy, but he took heed to the counsel of the nobleman, and never let the casket out of his hand.

'After my death you shall have everything, but I won't give it you now, for who knows what may happen? I have seen already how you treated your old father when he had nothing. It shall all be yours, I say, only wait; and when I die, take it and divide it as I have said.'

So, the brothers tended their father, and the old man lived in clover, and was somebody. He had his own way and did nothing.

So, the old man was no longer ill-treated by his children, but lived among them like an emperor in his own empire, but no sooner did he die than his children made what haste they could to lay hands upon the casket. All the people were called together and bore witness that they had treated their father well since he came back to them, so it was adjudged that they should divide the treasure amongst them. But first they took the old man's body to church and the casket along with it. They buried him as God commands. They made a rich banquet of funeral meats that all might know how much they mourned the old man; it was a splendid funeral.

When the priest got up from the table, the people all began to thank their hosts, and the eldest son begged the priest to say the sorokoust (a 40-day prayer) in the church for the repose of the dead man's soul. 'Such a dear old fellow as he was!' said he; 'was there ever anyone like him? Take this money for the sorokoust, reverend father!' so horribly grieved was that eldest son. So, the eldest son gave the priest money, and the second son gave him the like. Nay, each one gave him money for an extra half sorokoust, all four gave him requiem money.

'We'll have prayers in church for our father though we sell our last sheep to pay for them,' cried they.

Then, when all was over, they hastened as fast as they could to the money.

The coffer was brought forth. They shook it. There was a fine rattling inside it. Every one of them felt and handled the coffer. That was something like a treasure! Then they unsealed it and opened it and scattered the contents – and it was full of nothing but glass! They wouldn't believe their eyes. They rummaged among the glass, but there was no money. It was horrible! Surely it could not be that their father had dug up a coffer from beneath an oak of the forest and it was full of nothing but glass!

'Why!' cried the brothers, 'our father has left us nothing but glass!' But for the crowds of people there, the brothers would have fallen upon and beaten each other in their wrath. So, the children of the old man saw that their father had made fools of them.

Then all the people mocked them: 'You see what you have gained by sending your father to school! You see he learned something at school after all! He was a long time before he began learning, but better late than never. It appears to us 'twas a right good school you sent him to. No doubt they whipped him into learning so much. Never mind, you can keep the money and the casket!'

Then the brothers were full of lamentation and rage. But what could they do? Their father was already dead and buried.

From: Cossack Fairy Tales & Folk Tales

The Beautiful Daughter of Liu-Kung

IN ONE OF the central provinces of this long-lived Empire of China, there lived in very early times a man of the name of Chan. He was a person of a bright, active nature which made him enjoy life, and caused him to be popular amongst his companions and a favourite with everyone who knew him. But he was also a scholar, well-versed in the literature of his country, and he spent every moment that he could spare in the study of the great writings of the famous men of former days.

In order that he might be interrupted as little as possible in his pursuit of learning, he engaged a room in a famous monastery some miles away from his own home. The only inhabitants of this monastery were a dozen or so of Buddhist priests who, except when they were engaged in the daily services of the temple, lived a quiet, humdrum, lazy kind of existence which harmonized well with the solitude and the majestic stillness of the mountain scenery by which they were surrounded.

This monastery was indeed one of the most beautiful in China. It was situated on the slope of a hill, looking down upon a lovely valley, where the natural solitude was as complete as the most devoted hermit could desire. The only means of getting to it were the narrow hill footpaths along which the worshippers from the great city and the scattered villages wound in and out on festal days, when they came trooping to the temple to make their offerings to the famous God enshrined within.

Chan was a diligent student, and rarely indulged in recreation of any kind. Occasionally, when his mind became oppressed with excessive study he would go for a quiet walk along the hillside; but these occasions were few and far between, for he made up for every hour he spent away from his beloved books by still closer application to them in the hours that followed.

One day, he was strolling in an aimless kind of way on the hillside, when suddenly a party of hunters from the neighbouring city of Eternal Spring came dashing into view. They were a merry group and full of excitement, for they had just sighted a fox which Chan had seen a moment before flying away at its highest speed in mortal dread of its pursuers.

Prominent amongst the hunters was a young girl who was mounted on a fiery little steed, so full of spirit and so eager to follow in the mad chase after the prey that its rider seemed to have some difficulty in restraining it. The girl herself was a perfect picture. Her face was the loveliest that Chan had ever looked upon, and her figure, which her trim hunting dress showed off to the utmost advantage, was graceful in the extreme. As she swept by him with her face flushed with excitement and her features all aglow with health, Chan felt at once that he had lost his heart and that he was deeply and profoundly in love with her.

On making enquiries, he found that she was named Willow, that she was the daughter of the chief mandarin of the town in which she lived, and that she was intensely fond of the chase and delighted in galloping over the hills and valleys in the pursuit of the wild animals to be found there. So powerfully had Chan's mind been affected by what he had seen of Willow, that he had already begun to entertain serious thoughts of making her his wife; but while his mind was full of this delightful prospect, he was plunged into the deepest grief by hearing that she had suddenly died. For some days, he was so stricken with sorrow that he lost all interest in life and could do nothing but dwell on the memory of her, whom he had come to love with all the devotion of his heart.

A few weeks after the news of her death, the quiet of the retreat was one day broken by a huge procession which wound its way along the mountain path leading to the monastery doors. On looking out, Chan saw that many of the men in this procession were dressed in sackcloth, and that in front of it was a band of musicians producing weird, shrill notes on their various instruments.

By these signs, Chan knew that what he saw was a funeral, and he expected to see the long line of mourners pass on to some spot on the hillside where the dead would be buried. Instead of that, however, they entered through the great gates of the monastery, and the coffin, the red pall of which told him that it contained the body of a woman, was carried into an inner room of the building and laid on trestles that had been made ready for it.

After the mourners had dispersed, Chan asked one of the priests the name of the woman who had died, and how it was that the coffin was laid within the precincts of the temple instead of in the house of the deceased, where it could be looked after by her relatives and where the customary sacrifices to the spirit of the dead could be offered more conveniently than in the monastery.

The bonze replied that this was a peculiar case, calling for special treatment.

'The father of the poor young girl who died so suddenly,' he said, 'was the mandarin of the neighbouring city of Eternal Spring. Just after the death of his daughter, an order came from the Emperor transferring him to another district, a thousand miles from here.

'The command was very urgent that he should proceed without delay to take up his post in the far-off province, and that he was to allow nothing to hinder him from doing so. He could not carry his daughter's body with him on so long a journey, and no time was permitted him to take the coffin to his home, where she might be buried amongst her own kindred. It was equally impossible to deposit the coffin in the yamen he was about to leave, for the new mandarin who was soon to arrive would certainly object to have the body of a stranger in such close proximity to his family. It might bring him bad luck, and his career as an official might end in disaster.

'Permission was therefore asked from our abbot to allow the coffin to be placed in one of our vacant rooms until the father some day in the future can come and bear the body of his beloved daughter to the home of his ancestors, there to be laid at rest amongst his own people.

'This request was readily granted, for whilst he was in office, the mandarin showed us many favours, and his daughter was a beautiful girl who was beloved by everyone; and so we were only too glad to do anything in our power to help in this unhappy matter.'

Chan was profoundly moved when he realized that the woman whom he had loved as his own life lay dead within a chamber only a few steps away from his own. His passion, instead of being crushed out of his heart by the thought that she was utterly beyond his reach, and by no possibility could ever be more to him than a memory, seemed to grow in intensity as he became conscious that it was an absolutely hopeless one.

On that very same evening, about midnight, when silence rested on the monastery, and the priests were all wrapped in slumber, Chan, with a lighted taper in his hand, stole with noiseless footsteps along the dark passages into the chamber of death where his beloved lay. Kneeling beside the coffin with a heart full of emotion, in trembling accents he called upon Willow to listen to the story of his passion.

He spoke to her just as though she were standing face to face with him, and he told her how he had fallen in love with her on the day on which he had caught a glimpse of her as she galloped in pursuit of the fox that had fled through the valley from the hunters. He had planned, he told her, to make her his wife, and he described, in tones through which the tears could be heard to run, how heart-broken he was when he heard of her death.

'I want to see you,' he continued, 'for I feel that I cannot live without you. You are near to me, and yet oh! how far away. Can you not come from the Land of Shadows, where you are now, and comfort me by one vision of your fair face, and one sound of the voice that would fill my soul with the sweetest music?'

For many months the comfort of Chan's life was this nightly visit to the chamber where his dead love lay. Not a single night passed without his going to tell her of the unalterable and undying affection that filled his heart; and whilst the temple lay shrouded in darkness, and the only sounds that broke the stillness were those inexplicable ones in which nature seems to indulge when man is removed by sleep from the scene, Chan was uttering those love notes which had lain deeply hidden within his soul, but which now in the utter desolation of his heart burst forth to ease his pain by their mere expression.

One night as he was sitting poring over his books, he happened to turn round, and was startled to see the figure of a young girl standing just inside the door of his room. It seemed perfectly human, and yet it was so ethereal that it had the appearance of a spirit of the other world. As he looked at the girl with a wondering gaze, a smile lit up her beautiful features, and he then discovered to his great joy that she was none other than Willow, his lost love whom he had despaired of ever seeing again.

With her face wreathed in smiles, she sat down beside him and said in a timid, modest way: 'I am here tonight in response to the great love which has never faltered since the day I died. That is the magnet which has had the power of drawing me from the Land of Shadows. I felt it there, and many speak about it in that sunless country. Even Yam-lo, the lord of the spirits of that dreary world, has been moved by your unchanging devotion; so much so that he has given me permission to come and see you, in order that I might tell you how deeply my heart is moved by the profound affection that you have exhibited for me all these months during which you never had any expectation of its being returned.'

For many months, this sweet intercourse between Chan and his beloved Willow was carried on, and no one in the whole monastery knew anything of it. The interviews always took place about midnight, and Willow, who seemed to pass with freedom through closed doors or the stoutest walls, invariably vanished during the small hours of the morning.

One evening whilst they were conversing on topics agreeable to them both, Willow unburdened her heart to Chan, and told him how unhappy she was in the world of spirits.

'You know,' she said, 'that before I died, I was not married, and so I am only a wandering spirit with no place where I can rest, and no friends to whom I can betake myself. I travel here and there and everywhere, feeling that no one cares for me, and that there are no ties to bind me to any particular place or thing. For a young girl like me, this is a very sad and sorrowful state of things.

'There is another thing that adds to my sorrow in the Land of Shadows,' she went on to say, with a mournful look on her lovely countenance. 'I was very fond of hunting when I was in my father's home, and many a wild animal was slain in the hunting expeditions in which I took an active part. This has all told against me in the world in which I am now living, and for the share I took in destroying life, I have to suffer by many pains and penalties which are hard for me to endure.

'My sin has been great,' she said, 'and so I wish to make special offerings in this temple to the Goddess of Mercy and implore her to send down to the other world a good report of me to Yam-lo and intercede with him to forgive the sins of which I have been guilty. If you will do this for me, I promise that after I have been born again into the world I will never forget you, and if you like to wait for me, I shall willingly become your wife and serve you with the deepest devotion of which my heart is capable, as long as Heaven will permit you and me to live together as husband and wife.'

From this time, much to the astonishment of the priests in the monastery, Chan began to show unwonted enthusiasm for the service of the Goddess and would sometimes spend hours before her image and repeat long prayers to her. This was all the more remarkable, as the scholar had rarely if ever shown any desire to have anything to do with the numerous gods which were enshrined in various parts of the temple.

After some months of this daily appeal to the Goddess of Mercy, Willow informed him that his prayers had been so far successful that the misery of her lot in the Land of Shadows had been greatly mitigated. The pleadings of the Goddess with Yam-lo had so influenced his heart towards Willow that she believed her great sin in the destruction of animal life had been forgiven, and there were signs that the dread ruler of the Underworld was looking upon her with kindness.

Chan was delighted with this news, and his prayers and offerings became still more frequent and more fervent. He little dreamed that his devotion to the Goddess would be the means of his speedy separation from Willow, but so it was. One evening, she came as usual to see him, but instead of entering with smiling face and laughter in her eyes, she was weeping bitterly as though she were in the direst sorrow.

Chan was in the greatest distress when he saw this and asked her to explain the reason for her grief.

'The reason for my tears,' she said, 'is because after this evening I shall not see you again. Your petitions to the Goddess have had such a powerful effect upon her mind that she has used all her influence with Yam-lo to induce him to set me free from the misery of the Land of Shadows, and so I am to leave that sunless country and to be born again into life in this upper world.'

As she uttered these words her tears began to flow once more and her whole frame was convulsed with sobbing.

'I am glad,' she said, 'that I am to be born once more and live amongst men, but I cannot bear the thought of having to be separated for so long from you. Let us not grieve too much, however. It is our fate, and we may not rebel against it. Yam-lo has been kinder to me than he has ever been to anyone in the past, for he has revealed to me the family into which I am to be born and the place where they live, so if you come to me in eighteen years you will find me waiting for you. Your love has been so great that it has entered into my very soul, and there is nothing that can ever efface it from my heart. A thousand re-births may take place, but never shall I love any one as I love you.'

94

Chan professed that he was greatly comforted by this confession of her love, but all the same he felt in despair when he thought of the future.

'When next I shall see you,' he said with a sigh, 'I shall be getting so old that you, a young girl in the first flush of womanhood, will not care to look at me. My hair will have turned grey and my face will be marked with wrinkles, and in the re-birth you will have forgotten all that took place in the Land of Shadows, and the memory of me will have vanished from your heart for ever.'

Willow looked with loving but sorrowful eyes upon her lover as he was expressing his concern about the future, but quickly assured him that nothing in the world would ever cause her to cease to remember him with the tenderest affection.

'In order to comfort you,' she said, 'let me tell you of two things that the dread Yam-lo, out of consideration for your love for me, has granted me – two things which he has never bestowed upon any other mortal who has come within the region of his rule. The first is, he has allowed me to inspect the book of Life and Death, in which is recorded the history of every human being, with the times of their re-births and the places in which they are to be born. I want you this very minute to write down the secret which has been revealed to me as to my new name and family and the place where I shall reside, so that you will have no difficulty in finding me, when eighteen years hence you shall come to claim me as your wife.

'The next is a gift so precious that I have no words in which to express my gratitude for its having been bestowed upon me. It is this: I am given the privilege of not forgetting what has taken place during my stay in the Land of Shadows, and so when I am re-born into another part of China, with a new father and mother, I shall hold within my memory my recollection of you. The years will pass quickly, for I shall be looking for you, and this day eighteen years hence will be the happiest in my life, for it will bring you to me never more to be separated from me.

'But I must hasten on,' she hurriedly exclaimed, 'for the footsteps of fate are moving steadily towards me. In a few minutes, the gates of Hades will have closed against me, and Willow will have vanished, and I shall be a babe once more with my new life before me. See, but a minute more is left me, and I seem to have so much to say. Farewell! Never forget me! I shall ever remember you, but my time is come!'

As she uttered these words, a smile of ineffable sweetness flashed across, her beautiful face, and she was gone.

Chan was inexpressibly sad at the loss he had sustained by the re-birth of Willow, and in order to drive away his sorrow he threw his heart and soul into his studies. His books became his constant companions, and he tried to find in them a solace for the loneliness which had come upon him since the visits of Willow had ceased. He also became a diligent worshipper of the idols, and especially of the Goddess of Mercy, who had played such an important part in the history of his beloved Willow.

The years went slowly by, and Chan began to feel that he was growing old. His hair became dashed with silver threads, and wrinkles appeared in his forehead and under his eyes. The strain of waiting for the one woman who had taken complete possession of his heart had been too much for him. As the time drew near, too, when he should go to meet her, a great and nervous dread began to fill him with anxiety. Would she recognize him? And would she, a young girl of eighteen, be content to accept as a husband a man so advanced in years as he now was? These questions were constantly flashing through his brain.

At last, only a few months remained before he was to set out on his journey to the distant province where Yam-lo had decided that Willow was to begin her new life on earth.

He was sitting one evening in his study, brooding over the great problem that would be solved before long, when a man dressed in black silently entered the room. Looking on Chan with a kindly smile which seemed to find its way instantly to his heart, he informed him that he was a fairy from the Western Heaven and that he had been specially deputed by the rulers there to render him all the assistance in his power at this particular crisis, when they knew his heart was so full of anxiety.

'We have all heard in that far-off fairyland,' he continued, 'of the devotion you have shown to Willow, and how during all the years which have intervened since you saw her last you have never faltered in your love for her. Such affection is rare among mortals, and the dwellers in fairyland would like to help in bringing together two such loving hearts; for let me assure you that however strong your feeling for the one whom you are so anxious to see again, she on her part is just as deeply in love with you, and is now counting the days until she will be able to see you and until you need never again be parted from each other. In order to assist in this happy consummation, I want you to take a short trip with me. It will only take a few hours, and you will then find that something has happened to remove all your fears as to how you will be received by Willow.'

The fairy man then led Chan to the door and gave a wave of his hand in the direction of the sky. Instantly, the sound of the fluttering and swish of wings was heard, and in a moment a splendid eagle landed gracefully at their feet. Taking their seats upon its back, they found themselves flashing at lightning speed away through the darkness of the night. Higher and higher they rose, till they had pierced the heavy masses of clouds which hung hovering in the sky. Swift as an arrow, the eagle still cleft its way upward until the clouds had vanished to an infinite distance below them; and still onward they were borne in the mighty stillness of an expanse where no human being had ever travelled before.

Chan felt his heart throb with a nervousness which he could not control. What if the bird should tire, he thought, and he should be dropped into the fathomless abyss below? Life's journey would then come to a tragic end. Where, too, was he being carried and how should he be ever able to return to his far-off home on the earth? He was becoming more and more agitated, when the fairy took hold of his hand and in a voice which at once stilled his fears, assured him that there was not the least danger in this journey through the air.

'We are as safe here,' he assured him, 'as though we were standing upon a mountain whose roots lie miles below the surface of the earth. And see,' he continued, pointing to something in the distance, 'we shall arrive at our destination in the course of a few seconds.'

True enough, he had hardly finished speaking when a land fairer than Chan had ever seen on earth or pictured in imagination loomed up suddenly in front of them; and before he could gather together his astonished thoughts, the eagle had landed them on its shores, and with outspread wings was soaring into the mystery of the unknown beyond.

The fairy now led Chan along a road surrounded by the most bewildering beauty. Rare flowers, graceful trees, and birds which made the groves resound with the sweetest music, were objects that kept his mind in one continual state of delight. Before long, they arrived in front of a magnificent palace, so grand and vast that Chan felt afraid to enter within its portals, or even tread the avenue leading up to it.

Once more, his companion relieved Chan's anxiety by assuring him that he was an expected guest, and that the Queen of this fairy country had sent him to earth specially to invite him to come and visit her, in order that she might bestow upon him a blessing which would enrich the whole of his life and would enable him to spend many happy years with her whom he had loved with such devotion.

Chan was ushered into a large reception hall, where he was met by a very stately lady, with a face full of benevolence, whom he at once recognized from the images he had often worshipped as the Goddess of Mercy. He was startled when he discovered in what august presence he was standing and began to tremble with excitement as he realized that here in actual life was the famous personage whose image was worshipped by the millions of China, and whose influence spread even into the Land of Shadows.

Seeing Chan's humility and evident terror of her, the Goddess spoke to him in a gentle, loving voice, and told him to have no fear, for she had summoned him to her presence not to rebuke but to comfort him.

'I know your story,' she said, 'and I think it is a beautiful one. Before I was raised to the high position I now occupy, I was at one time a woman like Willow, and I can sympathize with her in her devotion to you because of the wonderful love you have shown her from the first moment that you saw her.

'I know, too, your anxiety about your age, and your fear lest when Willow sees you with the marks of advancing years upon you, her love may die out and you will be left with your heart broken and in despair. I have foreseen this difficulty, and I am going to have it removed.

'The fairy who brought you here,' she continued, 'will now take you round the palace grounds, and if you will carry out my wishes, the fears which have been troubling you for years shall entirely vanish. You will then meet Willow with a heart as light as that of any man in the flush of youth, who awaits the coming of the bridal chair which bears his future wife to his home.'

Chan at once, without any hesitation, followed his guide through the spacious grounds which surrounded the palace, and was finally led to the edge of a beautiful little lake embowered amongst trees and ferns, and rare and fragrant flowers. It was the most exquisite scene on which his vision had ever rested.

With a kindly look at his companion, the fairy said, 'This beautiful piece of water goes by the name of the 'Fountain of Eternal Youth,' and it is the Queen's express desire that you should bathe in it.'

Quickly undressing, Chan plunged into the pool and for a moment sank beneath the surface of the waters. Emerging quickly from them, a delightful feeling of new-born strength seemed to be creeping in at every pore of his body. The sense of advancing age passed away, and the years of youth appeared to come back to him again. He felt as though he were a young man once more; for the weary doubts, which for some years past had made his footsteps lag, had gone with his first plunge into those fragrant waters.

By-and-by he came out of this 'Fountain of Eternal Youth' with the visions and ambitions of his young manhood rushing through his brain. His powers, which seemed of late to have become dull and sluggish, had recovered the impetus which in earlier years had carried him so successfully through many a severe examination. His thoughts, too, about Willow had so completely changed that instead of dreading the day when he should stand before her, his one passionate desire now was to start upon his journey to keep his appointment with her.

Chan and the fairy then proceeded to the edge of the vast and boundless expanse which bordered the palace of the Goddess and found a magnificent dragon waiting to convey them back to earth. No sooner had they taken their seats on its back than it fled with the swiftness of the wind through the untrodden spaces of the air, until at length the mountains came looming out of the dim and shadowy distance, and with a rush Chan found himself safely landed at the door of the temple from which he had taken his departure for his amazing journey to the Western Heaven.

Whilst these wonderful things were taking place, Willow – or rather Precious Pearl, as she had been named by her new parents, who of course had no knowledge of her previous history – had grown up to be a most beautiful and fascinating woman.

During all these years, she had never ceased to look forward with an anxious heart to the day when she would once more meet the man to whom she had betrothed herself eighteen years ago. Latterly she had begun to count the days that must still elapse before she could see him again. She never forgot the night in the temple when she bade him 'Goodbye' just before she was reborn into this world. The day and the hour had been stamped upon her memory, and since then the years had seemed to travel with halting, leaden feet, as though they were loath to move on. But now only a few months remained, and no doubt ever entered her brain that Chan would fail her.

Just about this time her mother had an offer of marriage for her from a very wealthy and distinguished family, and contrary to the usual custom of mothers in China she asked her daughter what she thought of the proposal. Pearl was distressed beyond measure, and prayed and entreated her mother on no account to broach the subject to her again, as she could never entertain any proposition of the kind.

Amazed at such a statement, her mother begged her to explain her reason for such strange views.

'Girls at your age,' she said, 'are usually betrothed and are thinking of having homes of their own. This is the universal custom throughout the Empire, and therefore there must be some serious reason why you will not allow me to make arrangements for your being allied to some respectable family.'

Pearl had been feeling that the time was drawing near when she would have to divulge the secret of her love affair, and she considered that now was the best opportunity for doing so. To the astonishment therefore of her mother, who believed that she was romancing, she told her the whole story of the past; how Chan had fallen in love with her, and how after she had died and had come under the control of Yam-lo in the Land of Shadows, that dread lord had permitted her spirit to visit her lover in the temple where her body had been laid until a lucky resting-place could be found for it on the hillside. She also explained how it had been agreed between them that she was to wait for him until after the lapse of eighteen years, when she would be old enough to become his wife.

'In a few months the time will be up,' she concluded, 'and so I beseech you not to speak of my being betrothed to anyone else, for I feel that if I am compelled to marry any other than Chan I shall die.'

The mother was thunderstruck at this wonderful story which her daughter told her. She could only imagine that Pearl had in some way or another been bewitched, and was under a fatal delusion that she was in love with some hero of romance, to whom she believed she was betrothed. Still, her daughter had always been most loving and devoted to her and had shown more brightness and ability than Chinese girls of her age usually possessed. Her mother did not like, therefore, to reprove her for what she considered her ridiculous ideas, so she determined to try another plan to cure her of her folly.

'What age was this man Chan,' she asked, 'when you entered into this engagement with him?'

'He was just thirty,' Pearl replied.

'He was of very good family, and a scholar and had distinguished himself for his proficiency in the ancient literature of China.'

'Oh! then he must be nearly fifty now. A fine mate he would make for you, a young girl of only eighteen! But who knows how he may have changed since last you saw him? His hair must be turning grey, and his teeth may have fallen out; and for anything you know he may have been dead and buried so long ago that by this time they have taken up his bones, and nothing is left of him but what the funeral urn may contain of his ashes.'

'Oh! I do pray that nothing of that kind has happened to him,' cried Pearl, in a tone of voice which showed the anguish she was suffering. 'Let us leave the question for a few months, and then when he comes for me, as I know he will, you will find by personal knowledge what a splendid man he is, and how entirely worthy he is of being your son-in-law.'

On the day which had been appointed under such romantic circumstances eighteen years before, Chan arrived in the town, and after taking a room in an inn and making certain enquiries, he made his way to the home where he believed that Willow resided. On his arrival, however, he was roughly told by the servant that no such person as Willow lived there, and that they did not like strangers coming about the house. Indeed, he was given plainly to understand that the sooner he left, the better everyone would be pleased. This treatment was of course part of a scheme devised by Pearl's parents to frustrate any plans that Chan might have formed for seeing her. They were determined not to give their daughter to a man so old as he must be, and therefore they decided that an interview between the two must be prevented at all hazards.

Chan was greatly distressed at the rebuff which he had received. Had Willow after all made a mistake eighteen years ago when she gave him the name of this town as the place where her new home was to be? He had carefully written it down at her dictation, and it had been burned into his brain all the years since. No, there could be no mistake on that point. If there were any, then it was one that had been made purposely by Yam-lo in order to deceive them both. That idea, however, was unthinkable, and so there must be something else to account for his not finding Willow as he had expected. He at once made enquiries at the inn at which he was staying and found that there was a daughter at the very house to which he had gone, and that in almost every particular the description he was given of her corresponded with his beloved Willow.

In the meantime, poor Pearl was in a state of the greatest anxiety. The eventful day on which she was to meet her lover had opened for her with keen expectation of meeting him after their long and romantic separation. She had never for one moment doubted that he would keep his engagement with her. An instinct which she could not explain made her feel certain that he was still alive, and that nothing in the world would prevent him from meeting her, as had been agreed upon between them at that eventful parting in the temple eighteen years before.

As the day wore on, however, and there were no signs of Chan, Pearl's distress became exceedingly pitiful; and when night came and her mother declared that nothing had been seen of him, she was so stricken with despair that she lost all consciousness, and had to be carried to bed, where she lay in a kind of trance from which, for some time, it seemed impossible to arouse her.

When at last she did regain consciousness, her mother tried to comfort her by saying that perhaps Chan was dead, or that he had forgotten her in the long course of years, and that therefore she must not grieve too much.

'You are a young girl,' she said, 'and you have a long life before you. Chan is an old man by this time; no doubt he has long ago married, and the home ties which he has formed have caused him to forget you. But you need not be broken-hearted on that account. There are many other men who will be more suitable for you than he could possibly be. By-and-by we shall arrange a marriage for you, and then life will appear to you very different from what it does now.'

Instead of being comforted, however, Pearl was only the more distressed by her mother's words. Her love, which had begun in the Land of Shadows, and which had been growing in her heart for the last eighteen years, was not one to be easily put aside by such plausible arguments as those she had just listened to. The result was that she had a relapse, and for several days her life was in great danger.

The father and mother, fearing now that their daughter would die, determined, as there seemed no other remedy, to bring Chan to their home, and see whether his presence would not deliver Pearl from the danger in which the doctor declared she undoubtedly was.

The father accordingly went to the inn where he knew Chan was staying, and to his immense surprise he found him to be a young man of about twenty-five, highly polished in manner, and possessed of unusual intelligence. For some time, he utterly refused to believe that this handsome young fellow was really the man with whom Pearl was so deeply in love, and it was not until Chan had told him the romantic story of his life that he could at all believe that he was not being imposed upon. Eventually, however, he was so taken with Chan that he became determined to do all in his power to bring about his marriage with his daughter.

'Come with me at once,' he said, 'and see if your presence will not do more than the cleverest doctors in the town have been able to accomplish. Pearl has been so distressed at not seeing you that she is now seriously ill, and we have been afraid that she would die of a broken heart.'

When they arrived at the house Chan was taken into the sick-room, and the girl gazed into his face with a look of wonderment.

'I do not seem to recognize you,' she said in a feeble voice. 'You are much younger than Chan, and although there is something about you that reminds me of him, I cannot realize that you are the same person with whom my spirit eighteen years ago held fellowship in the monastery where my body lay unburied.'

Chan proceeded to explain the mystery.

'For years,' he said, 'my mind was troubled about the difference between our ages. I was afraid that when you saw me with grey hairs and with wrinkles on my face, your love would receive a shock, and you might regret that you had ever pledged yourself to me. Although you had vanished from my sight, my prayers still continued to be offered to the Goddess of Mercy. She had heard them for you, you remember, when you were in the Land of Shadows, and through her intercession Yam-lo had forgiven your sins and had made life easier for you in that gloomy country.

'I still continued to pray to her, hoping in some vague way that she would intervene to bring about the desire of my heart, and that when in due time I should meet you again, every obstacle to our mutual love would be for ever removed.

'One day, a fairy came into the very room where your spirit had often conversed with me. He carried me away with him to the Western Heaven and brought me into the very presence of the Goddess of Mercy. She gave directions for me to bathe in the 'Fountain of Eternal Youth,' and I became young again. That is why you see me now with a young face and a young nature, but my heart in its love for you has never changed, and never will as long as life lasts.'

As he was telling this entrancing story, a look of devoted love spread over the beautiful countenance of Pearl. She gradually became instilled with life, and before he had finished speaking, the lassitude and exhaustion which had seemed to threaten her very life entirely disappeared. A rosy look came over her face, and her coal-black eyes flashed with hidden fires.

'Now I know,' she cried, 'that you are Chan. You are so changed that when I first caught sight of you my heart sank within me, for I had pictured an older man, and I could not at once realize that you were the same Chan who showed such unbounded love for me in the years gone by.

'It was not that I should have loved you less even though you had really been older. My heart would never have changed. It was only my doubt as to your reality that made me hesitate, but now my happiness is indeed great; for since through the goodness of the Goddess you have recovered your youth, I need not fear that the difference between our years may in the near future bring to us an eternal separation.'

In a few days, Pearl was once more herself again. Her parents, delighted with the romantic turn that things had taken and highly pleased with Chan himself, arranged for the betrothal of their daughter to him; and in the course of a few months, the loving couple were united in marriage. And so, after years of waiting, the happy consummation was accomplished, which Heaven and the Goddess of Mercy and even the dread Ruler of the Land of Shadows had each taken a share in bringing about; and for many and many a long year the story of Chan and his wife was spread abroad throughout the region in which they lived.

From: Chinese Folk-lore Tales

Billy Duffy & the Devil

BILLY DUFFY WAS an Irishman, a blacksmith and a drunkard. He had the Celtic aversion of steady work, and stuck to his forge only long enough to get money for drink; when that was spent, he returned to work.

Billy was coming home one day after one of these drinking-bouts, soberer than usual, when he exclaimed to himself, for the thirst was upon him, 'By God! I would sell myself to the devil if I could get some more drink.'

At that moment a tall gentleman in black stepped up to him, and said, 'What did you say?'

'I said I would sell myself to the devil if I could get a drink.'

'Well, how much do you want for seven years, and the devil to get you then?'

'Well, I can't tell exactly, when it comes to the push.'

'Will £700 do you?'

'Yes; I'd take £700.'

'And the devil to get you then?'

'Oh, yes; I don't care about that.'

When Billy got home, he found the money in his smithy. He at once shut the smithy, and began squandering the money, keeping open house.

Amongst the people who flocked to get what they could out of Billy came an old hermit, who said, 'I am very hungry, and nearly starved. Will you give me something to eat and drink?'

'Oh, yes; come in and get what you like.'

The hermit disappeared, after eating and drinking, and did not reappear for several months, when he received the same kindly welcome, again disappearing. A few months afterwards he again appeared.

'Come in, come in!' said Billy.

After he had eaten and drunk his full, the hermit said to Billy: 'Well, three times have you been good and kind to me. I'll give you three wishes, and whatever you wish will be sure to come true.'

'I must have time to consider,' said Billy.

'Oh, you shall have plenty of time to consider, and mind they are good wishes.'

Next morning Billy told the hermit he was ready.

'Well, go on; be sure they're good wishes,' said the hermit.

'Well, I've got a big sledgehammer in the smithy, and I wish whoever gets hold of that hammer shall go on striking the anvil, and never break it, till I tell him to stop.'

'Oh, that's a bad wish, Billy.'

'Oh, no; you'll see it's good. Next thing I wish for is a purse so that no one can take out whatever I put into it.'

'Oh, Billy, Billy! that's a bad wish. Be careful now about the third wish,' said the hermit.

'Well, I have got an armchair upstairs, and I wish that whoever may sit in that armchair will never be able to get up till I let them.'

'Well, well, indeed; they are not very good wishes.'

'Oh, yes; I've got my senses about me. I think I'll make them good wishes, after all.'

The seven years, all but three days, had passed, and Billy was back working at his forge, for all his money was gone, when the dark gentleman stepped in and said: 'Now, Billy, during these last three days you may have as much money as you like,' and he disappeared.

On the last day of his seven years Billy was penniless, and he went to the taproom of his favourite inn, which was full.

'Well, boys,' said Billy, 'we must have some money tonight. I'll treat you, and give you a pound each,' and rising, he placed his tumbler in the middle of the table and wished for twenty pounds. No sooner had he wished than a ball of fire came through the ceiling, and the twenty sovereigns fell into the tumbler. Everyone was taken aback, and there was a noise as if a bomb had burst, and the fireball disappeared, and rolled down the garden path, the landlord following it. After this they each drank what they liked, and Billy gave them a sovereign apiece before he went home.

The next morning, he was in his smithy making a pair of horseshoes, when the devil came in and said: 'Well, Billy, I'll want you this morning.'

'Yes; all right. Take hold of this sledge-hammer and give me a few hammers till I finish this job before I go.'

So, the devil seized the hammer and began striking the anvil, but he couldn't stop.

So, Billy laughed, and locked him in, and was away three days. During this time, the people collected round the smithy, and peeped through the cracks in the shutter, for they could hear the hammer going night and day.

At the end of three days Billy returned and opened the door, and the devil said, 'Oh, Billy, you've played a fine trick to me; let me go.'

'What are you going to give me if I let you go?'

'Seven years more, twice the money, and two days' grace for wishing for what you like.'

The devil paid his money and disappeared, and Billy shut the smithy and took to gambling and drinking, so that at the end of seven years he was without a penny and working again in his smithy.

On the last night of the seven years, he went to his favourite public house again, and wished for five pounds.

After he wished, a little man entered and spat the sovereigns into the tumbler, and they all drank all night.

Next morning, Billy went back to his smithy. The devil, who had grown suspicious, turned himself into a sovereign and appeared on the floor. Billy seized the sovereign and clapped it into his purse. Then he took his purse and lay it upon the anvil, and began to beat it with his sledgehammer, when the devil began to call out, 'Spare my poor limbs, spare my poor limbs!'

'How much now if I let you go?' asked Billy

'Seven more years, three times the money, and one day in which to wish for what you like.'

Billy took the sovereign out of his purse and threw it away, when he found his money in the smithy.

Billy carried on worse than ever; gambled and drank and raced, squandering it all before his seven years was gone. On the last day of his term, he went to his favourite inn as usual and wished for a tumbler full of sovereigns. A little man with a big head, a big nose, and big mouth, a little body, and little legs, with clubbed feet and a forked tail, brought them in and put them in the tumbler. The drunkards in the room got scared when they saw the little man, for he looked all glowing with fire as he danced on the table.

When he finished, he said, 'Billy, tomorrow morning our compact is up.'

'I know it, old boy, I know it, old boy!' said Billy.

Then the devil ran out and disappeared, and the people began to question Billy: 'What is that? I think it is you, Mister Duffy, he is after.'

'Oh, it is nothing at all,' said Billy.

'I should think there was something,' said the man.

'I am afraid my house will get a bad name,' croaked the landlord.

'Not in the least! You are only a coward,' said Billy.

'But in the name of God, what is it all about?' asked an old man.

'Oh, you'll see by-and-bye,' said Billy; 'it is nothing at all.'

Next morning Billy went to his smithy, but the devil would not come near it.

So he went to his house, and began to quarrel with his wife, and whilst he was quarrelling the devil walked in and said: 'Well, Mr. Duffy, I am ready for you.'

'Ah, yes; just sit down and wait a minute or two. I have some papers I want to put to rights before I go.'

So, the devil sat down in the arm-chair, and Billy went to the smithy and heated a pair of tongs red-hot, and coming back, he got the devil by the nose, and pulled it out as though it had been soft iron. And the devil began yelling, but he could not move, and Billy kept drawing the nose out till it was long enough to reach over the window, when he put an old bell-topper on the end of it. And the devil yelled, and snorted fire from his nose.

The whole of the village crowded round Billy's, house – at a safe distance – calling out, 'Billy and the devil! The devil and Billy Duffy!'

The devil got awful savage, and blackguarded Billy Duffy terribly; but it was useless. Billy kept him there for days, till he got civil and said: 'Mr. Duffy, what will you let me go for?'

'Only one thing: I am to live the rest of my life without you and have as much gold as I like.'

The devil agreed, so Billy let him go; and immediately he grew rich. He lived to a good old age squandering money all the time, but at last he died and when he got to the gates of hell the clerk said, 'Who are you?'

'Billy Duffy,' said he.

And when the devil, who was standing near, heard, he said: 'Good God! Bar the gates and double-lock them, for if this Billy Duffy the blacksmith gets in he will ruin us all.'

Old Billy saw a pair of red-hot tongs, which he picked up, and seized the devil by the nose. When the devil pulled back his head, he left a red-hot bit of his nose in the tongs.

Then Billy Duffy went up to the gates of heaven and St. Peter asked him who he was.

'Billy Duffy the blacksmith,' he answered.

'No admittance! You are a bold, bad man,' said St. Peter.

'Good God! What will I do?' said Billy, and he went back to the earth, where he and the piece of the devil's nose melted into a ball of fire, and he roves the earth till this day as a will-o'-the-wisp.

From: Welsh Fairy-Tales & Other Stories

Prince Hyacinth & the Dear Little Princess

ONCE UPON A time, there lived a King who was deeply in love with a Princess, but she could not marry anyone, because she was under an enchantment. So, the King set out to seek a fairy, and asked what he could do to win the Princess's love.

The Fairy said to him: 'You know that the Princess has a great cat which she is very fond of. Whoever is clever enough to tread on that cat's tail is the man she is destined to marry.'

The King said to himself that this would not be very difficult; and he left the Fairy, determined to grind the cat's tail to powder rather than not tread on it at all.

You may imagine that it was not long before he went to see the Princess; and puss, as usual, marched in before him, arching its back. The King took a long step, and quite thought he had the tail under his foot, but the cat turned round so sharply that he trod only on air. And so, it went on for eight days, till the King began to think that this fatal tail must be full of quicksilver – it was never still for a moment.

At last, however, he was lucky enough to come upon puss fast asleep and with its tail conveniently spread out. So, the King, without losing a moment, set his foot upon it heavily.

With one terrific yell the cat sprang up and instantly changed into a tall man, who, fixing his angry eyes upon the King, said: 'You shall marry the Princess because you have been able to break the enchantment, but I will have my revenge. You shall have a son, who will never be happy until he finds out that his nose is too long, and if you ever tell anyone what I have just said to you, you shall vanish away instantly, and no one shall ever see you or hear of you again.'

Though the King was horribly afraid of the enchanter, he could not help laughing at this threat.

'If my son has such a long nose as that,' he said to himself, 'he must always see it or feel it; at least, if he is not blind or without hands.'

But, as the enchanter had vanished, he did not waste any more time in thinking, but went to seek the Princess, who very soon consented to marry him. But after all, they had not been married very long when the King died, and the Queen had nothing left to care for but her little son, who was called Hyacinth. The little Prince had large blue eyes, the prettiest eyes in the world, and a sweet little mouth, but alas! His nose was so enormous that it covered half his face. The Queen was inconsolable when she saw this great nose, but her ladies assured her that it was not really as large as it looked; that it was a Roman nose, and you had only to open any history book to see that every hero has a large nose. The Queen, who was devoted to her baby, was pleased with what they told her, and when she looked at Hyacinth again, his nose certainly did not seem to her quite so large.

The Prince was brought up with great care; and, as soon as he could speak, they told him all sorts of dreadful stories about people who had short noses. No one was allowed to come near him whose nose did not more or less resemble his own, and the courtiers, to get into favour with the Queen, took to pulling their babies' noses several times every day to make them grow long. But, do what they would, they were nothing by comparison with the Prince's.

When he grew older, he learned history; and whenever any great prince or beautiful princess was spoken of, his teachers took care to tell him that they had long noses.

His room was hung with pictures, all of people with very large noses; and the Prince grew up so convinced that a long nose was a great beauty that he would not on any account have had his own a single inch shorter!

When his twentieth birthday was past, the Queen thought it was time that he should be married, so she commanded that the portraits of several princesses should be brought for him to see, and among the others was a picture of the Dear Little Princess!

Now, she was the daughter of a great King, and would someday possess several kingdoms herself; but Prince Hyacinth had not a thought to spare for anything of that sort, he was so much struck with her beauty. The Princess, whom he thought quite charming, had, however, a little saucy nose, which, in her face, was the prettiest thing possible, but it was a cause of great embarrassment to the courtiers, who had got into such a habit of laughing at little noses that they sometimes found themselves laughing at hers before they had time to think. But this did not do at all before the Prince, who quite failed to see the joke, and actually banished two of his courtiers who had dared to mention disrespectfully the Dear Little Princess's tiny nose!

The others, taking warning from this, learned to think twice before they spoke, and one even went so far as to tell the Prince that, though it was quite true that no man could be worth anything unless he had a long nose, still, a woman's beauty was a different thing, and he knew a learned man who understood Greek and had read in some old manuscripts that the beautiful Cleopatra herself had a 'tip-tilted' nose!

The Prince made him a splendid present as a reward for this good news, and at once sent ambassadors to ask the Dear Little Princess in marriage. The King, her father, gave his consent; and Prince Hyacinth, who, in his anxiety to see the Princess, had gone three leagues to meet her, was just advancing to kiss her hand when, to the horror of all who stood by, the enchanter appeared as suddenly as a flash of lightning, and, snatching up the Dear Little Princess, whirled her away out of their sight!

The Prince was left quite inconsolable, and declared that nothing should induce him to go back to his kingdom until he had found her again, and refusing to allow any of his courtiers to follow him, he mounted his horse and rode sadly away, letting the animal choose its own path.

So it happened that he came presently to a great plain, across which he rode all day long without seeing a single house, and horse and rider were terribly hungry, when, as the night fell, the Prince caught sight of a light.

He rode up to it, and saw a little old woman, who appeared to be at least a hundred years old. She put on her spectacles to look at Prince Hyacinth, but it was quite a long time before she could fix them securely, because her nose was so very short.

The Prince and the Fairy (for that was who she was) had no sooner looked at one another than they went into fits of laughter, and cried at the same moment, 'Oh, what a funny nose!'

'Not so funny as your own,' said Prince Hyacinth to the Fairy; 'but, madam, I beg you to leave the consideration of our noses – such as they are – and to be good enough to give me something to eat, for I am starving, and so is my poor horse.'

'With all my heart!' said the Fairy. 'Though your nose is so ridiculous, you are, nevertheless, the son of my best friend. I loved your father as if he had been my brother. Now he had a very handsome nose!'

'And pray, what does mine lack?' said the Prince.

'Oh! it doesn't lack anything,' replied the Fairy. 'On the contrary quite, there is only too much of it. But never mind, one may be a very worthy man though his nose is too long. I was telling you that I was your father's friend; he often came to see me in the old times, and you must know that I was very pretty in those days; at least, he used to say so. I should like to tell you of a conversation we had the last time I ever saw him.'

'Indeed,' said the Prince, 'when I have supped it will give me the greatest pleasure to hear it; but consider, madam, I beg of you, that I have had nothing to eat today.'

'The poor boy is right,' said the Fairy; 'I was forgetting. Come in, then, and I will give you some supper, and while you are eating, I can tell you my story in a very few words – for I don't like endless tales myself. Too long a tongue is worse than too long a nose, and I remember when I was young that I was so much admired for not being a great chatterer. They used to tell the Queen, my mother, that it was so. For though you see what I am now, I was the daughter of a great king. My father – '

'Your father, I dare say, got something to eat when he was hungry!' interrupted the Prince.

'Oh! Certainly,' answered the Fairy, 'and you also shall have supper directly. I only just wanted to tell you – '

'But I really cannot listen to anything until I have had something to eat,' cried the Prince, who was getting quite angry; but then, remembering that he had better be polite as he much needed the Fairy's help, he added: 'I know that in the pleasure of listening to you I should quite forget my own hunger; but my horse, who cannot hear you, must really be fed!'

The Fairy was very much flattered by this compliment, and said, calling to her servants: 'You shall not wait another minute, you are so polite, and in spite of the enormous size of your nose you are really very agreeable.'

'Plague take the old lady! How she does go on about my nose!' said the Prince to himself. 'One would almost think that mine had taken all the extra length that hers lacks! If I were not so hungry, I would soon have done with this chatterpie who thinks she talks very little! How stupid people are not to see their own faults! That comes of being a princess; she has been spoilt by flatterers, who have made her believe that she is quite a moderate talker!'

Meanwhile the servants were putting the supper on the table, and the Prince was much amused to hear the Fairy, who asked them a thousand questions simply for the pleasure of hearing herself speak; especially he noticed one maid who, no matter what was being said, always contrived to praise her mistress's wisdom.

'Well!' he thought, as he ate his supper. 'I'm very glad I came here. This just shows me how sensible I have been in never listening to flatterers. People of that sort praise us to our faces without shame, and hide our faults or change them into virtues. For my part, I never will be taken in by them. I know my own defects, I hope.'

Poor Prince Hyacinth! He really believed what he said and hadn't an idea that the people who had praised his nose were laughing at him, just as the Fairy's maid was laughing at her; for the Prince had seen her laugh slyly when she could do so without the Fairy's noticing her.

However, he said nothing, and presently, when his hunger began to be appeased, the Fairy said: 'My dear Prince, might I beg you to move a little more that way, for your nose casts such a shadow that I really cannot see what I have on my plate. Ah! Thanks. Now let us speak of your father. When I went to his Court, he was only a little boy, but that is forty years ago, and I have been in this desolate place ever since. Tell me what goes on nowadays; are the ladies as fond of amusement as ever? In my time one saw them at parties, theatres, balls, and promenades every day. Dear me! What a long nose you have! I cannot get used to it!'

'Really, madam,' said the Prince, 'I wish you would leave off mentioning my nose. It cannot matter to you what it is like. I am quite satisfied with it and have no wish to have it shorter. One must take what is given one.'

'Now you are angry with me, my poor Hyacinth,' said the Fairy, 'and I assure you that I didn't mean to vex you; on the contrary, I wished to do you a service. However, though I really cannot help your nose being a shock to me, I will try not to say anything about it. I will even try to think that you have an ordinary nose. To tell the truth, it would make three reasonable ones.'

The Prince, who was no longer hungry, grew so impatient at the Fairy's continual remarks about his nose that at last, he threw himself upon his horse and rode hastily away. But wherever he came in his journey he thought the people were mad, for they all talked of his nose, and yet he could not bring himself to admit that it was too long, he had been so used all his life to hear it called handsome.

The old Fairy, who wished to make him happy, at last hit upon a plan. She shut the Dear Little Princess up in a palace of crystal and put this palace down where the Prince could not fail to find it. His joy at seeing the Princess again was extreme, and he set to work with all his might to try to break her prison, but in spite of all his efforts he failed utterly. In despair he thought at least that he would try to get near enough to speak to the Dear Little Princess who, on her part, stretched out her hand that he might kiss it; but turn which way he might, he never could raise it to his lips, for his long nose always prevented it.

For the first time, he realized how long it really was, and exclaimed: 'Well, it must be admitted that my nose is too long!'

In an instant the crystal prison flew into a thousand splinters, and the old Fairy, taking the Dear Little Princess by the hand, said to the Prince: 'Now, say if you are not very much obliged to me. Much good it was for me to talk to you about your nose! You would never have found out how extraordinary it was if it hadn't hindered you from doing what you wanted to. You see how self-love keeps us from knowing our own defects of mind and body. Our reason tries in vain to show them to us; we refuse to see them till we find them in our way.'

Prince Hyacinth, whose nose was now just like anyone else's, did not fail to profit by the lesson he had received. He married the Dear Little Princess, and they lived happily ever after.

From: Boys & Girls Bookshelf Folk-Lore,
Fables, & Fairy Tales

Finis

Workbooks From The Scheherazade Foundation

We hope that you have enjoyed this collection of stories, gleaned from varying cultural corners of the world, and that you have been entertained by them.

But, have you considered the deeper meanings and interwoven layers that lie hidden beneath the surface?

At The Scheherazade Foundation, we believe that Teaching-Stories contain wisdom, information, and marvels that have the power to transform the way we think, and thereby change our lives.

Employed as a bedrock of culture throughout the centuries – challenging established patterns of thinking, while passing on knowledge and values – tales such as the ones contained in this volume are a rich resource ready and waiting to be mined.

As an aid to help in the perception of less-obvious facets and layers, we have created a series of original Workbooks. Aimed at stimulating thought-provoking discussions and igniting deep reflection, these tools will assist in unlocking the power of Teaching-Stories.